Death Over the Atlantic

ASHLEE BUTTERMAN

ISBN: 9798262540419

Contents

Chapter 1

The floor at the gate held a gloss that never looked clean, a shine over scuffs and shoe prints and a smear of soda near the trash can. Recycled air carried coffee and jet fuel and the dry bite of carpet cleaner. Amelia Hart checked the manifest on her tablet, pen tucked behind her ear, the world of departures and last-minute texts flowing around her like a tide that never reached her shoes.

"Good evening," she said, again and again, each greeting steady. She watched hands, eyes, the way people set down baggage, the small tells that said whether someone would need extra care at altitude.

The man with the velvet pouch stepped forward. Mid-forties. Gaunt cheeks. A tremor in his wrist that made the barcode on his

1

pass wobble when he held it out. The gate agent scanned: a small beep, then a nod. Lionel Hughes. His thumb stroked the pouch drawstring, and when the mouth of the bag opened a fraction, a coin flashed there, old metal with a rubbed rim and a nick near the top, a flaw at ten o'clock like a bite taken long ago.

"Boarding left side, Mr. Hughes," the agent said.

Lionel kept his chin low. A passenger behind him, tall with a hard set to his jaw, shifted and breathed through his nose like he had a list of grievances ready to file. Amelia let that pass without a hook. In a line at a gate, plenty of people bristled for sport.

"Welcome aboard," she said to Lionel.

He made himself meet her eyes. "Is it a full flight?"

"We'll make it work."

A smile touched his mouth but didn't stay. He moved on. The tall man followed, still tight, still measuring the world as if it owed him something and might pay tonight.

Amelia stepped to the jet bridge, collected two boarding stubs from the floor, and bent to pick up a torn scrap of paper flattened under a heel print. A faded line of ink ran through the grit. *old score*, then below it, *token*. She slid the scrap into her left uniform pocket, the pocket she used for stray claims that might matter later, and kept the stream of passengers flowing.

"First red-eye," a woman said, gripping her new husband's hand like it was a lifeline.

"You'll sleep," Amelia said.

"Will I?" the woman asked.

"Not a bet I can take," Amelia said, and the bride laughed with the kind of laugh that came from the throat, a soft relief.

At the door, Captain Reeves stepped out for thirty seconds to shake hands with a frequent flier who called him by first name and asked after his dog. Betsy Kwon waved like they were old pals. Reeves lifted a palm in greeting and went back into the fortified quiet of the cockpit.

Rows filled in waves. The push and give of human bodies trying to hang coats on air. Overheads clicked. A child asked if Paris had dragons. The child's mother said yes, polite ones. Deena, at the forward galley, rolled her shoulder and muttered about the turn time they'd been given on the last leg. "Ten minutes to reset a life," she said, not to anyone in particular.

Amelia moved the aisle. Check seat belts. Eyes on hands. A pair of whispered barbs at row twenty-one, not loud enough to quote later, sharp enough to draw a mental line under both faces. She logged Lionel in her head as 23D, aisle. He watched the aisle more than his screen, body angled as if ready to stand. The pouch sat in his lap. The coin's face caught a wash of light as the reading lamps settled. He kept glancing past his shoulder toward the mid-cabin, like a man with a promise he didn't trust.

Amelia kneeled at an armrest to steady a tray table latch, and there, wedged under a seat edge, she found the mate to the gate scrap: the same slanted hand, the same tired ink, the same diagonal tear across the corner. *an old score*, then farther along, *the token*. She slid the second piece into her left pocket with the first, two torn corners itching the same place on her palm through the fabric. She checked the row again, then stood.

The plane pushed back, that soft lurch like a shoulder bump. Lights dimmed for taxi. Outside, blue-white ramp lights smeared across the wet tarmac, thin rivulets moving with the push of air. Inside, the hush of a hundred private thoughts settled. The safety demo ran. Seat belts snapped. Hands reached for armrests, then pulled back for courtesy, then settled again when courtesy lost to need.

Roll. Engines rose to a steady pitch. Not loud, but present, a long chord under everything. The aircraft lifted and the city fell away. Up through cloud, then into night that looked like a wall until it didn't.

Amelia checked the bins one last time as the sign chimed off. Lionel tucked the coin into the velvet pouch with a care that read like reverence. On the far side of the aisle, a woman with a neat bun and a historian's posture, Dr. Greta Morrison by the manifest, watched the pouch without blinking, the way a curator watched a visitor hold a rare piece with unclean hands.

"Blanket when you can," Greta said.

"I'll bring one," Amelia said.

Betsy flagged Amelia with two fingers. "He keeps saying things," Betsy said, voice low. "Not to me. To the air. Something about family debts."

"Did you hear anything else?"

"Only that he's not sleeping," Betsy said. "He jumps when the cart squeaks. Like someone pressed a bruise."

"I'll check on him," Amelia said.

The first service pass began, a parade of choices that sounded simple and triggered three follow-up questions each. "Sparkling or still?" became a small referendum on life. Rita and Nolan debated aisle versus window like it was a pledge, and in the end decided to sit as assigned and hold hands across the armrest.

"You two okay?" Amelia asked.

"We're great," Rita said, and squeezed Nolan's fingers. "I mean, great enough."

"Great enough flies," Amelia said.

Row twenty-four held a minor disturbance. A man across the aisle leaned in to Amelia when she paused to set down a ginger ale. "He passed something to 24C," the man said, chin flicked toward Lionel.

"What did you see?"

"A handoff," the man said. "Small. Fast."

"What was it?"

"Could've been a coin," he said. "Could've been a cough drop."

The call light pinged from the forward lav. A child in first needed a different size of headphone jack and a firm word about kicking the seat. By the time Amelia turned back to 24C, six bodies and a cart blocked the angle. She made a note of the seat. She wrote it into the back of her mind as if ink would make it impossible to forget.

Later, with cups stacked and the aisle finally clear, she saw Lionel three rows ahead, leaned close to a figure tucked in the shadow at the curve of an overhead bin. The two had faces angled to avoid light. Lionel spoke into that shadow like a man at a confessional. When he lifted his head, his gaze met Amelia's. Whatever rose in him cut the words from his mouth. He pulled back. The figure shifted, then drifted into a seat before she could place the row with certainty.

She checked the time. She checked her left pocket. Two scraps rested there, paper against paper, their edges aligned by chance or design.

"Water?" she asked a nearby row.

"Yes, please," Greta said, eyes still set where the pouch had been.

Near the aft galley, Deena leaned on the counter for a breath. "Full moon of passengers," she said. "Every phase of humanity."

Amelia smiled, then didn't, then did again, because a smile mattered more than the fatigue that pressed between her shoulder blades.

She carried a blanket forward for Greta and found Lionel's row empty. His seatbelt strap lay coiled like a sleeping snake. She walked the aisle, found him near the mid-cabin door, hands under the velvet pouch as if it contained a heart.

"Sir," she said. "We'll keep aisles clear unless you're headed to the lav."

He nodded and went where she pointed. He took the pouch with him.

She wondered which gate agent had scanned him. Parker, she decided, the one who never bent a rule yet knew how to move a line.

The night smoothed. Cabin lights held to low. A soft clink of ice against plastic carried. A page turned. A whisper at the curtain to first. In a press of bodies, secrets traveled faster than carts.

Amelia lingered near row twenty-three. A woman in 22C asked for tea, and Amelia made it from memory, the way her mother had made it in the old apartment when storms came through and shook the window frame. Tea that tasted like better choices.

"Will we hit weather?" the woman asked.

"Nothing the captain hasn't already outflown," Amelia said.

A laugh from the rear reached forward. Betsy again, telling someone about a cat who learned to open her fridge at night and leave block letters in spilled flour. "It spelled 'feed me' once," she said. "We keep the flour in a bin now."

When Amelia turned, she saw Lionel again. He had returned to 23D, pouch in his lap. The coin lay in his palm, face up, the nick bright. He moved his thumb across it once, then tucked it away as if he feared even that touch would wear the edge thinner.

The world softened. The woman in 12A slept with her mouth open and her hand over her purse. The man in 14F typed a line, stared at it, deleted it, then stared harder. Footsteps behind curtains went still.

Amelia bent to secure a loose bag at her feet. A whisper up the aisle pulled her eyes. Lionel had leaned in again, this time to a figure who sat without a reading light. Another hushed exchange. He looked up. Their eyes met. Silence cut the thread. He leaned back and faced forward, shoulders squared, jaw set.

His abrupt quiet landed like a stone in water, and the rings spread all the way to Amelia's shoes.

She moved again, because movement kept the air from thinning. She had a note in her pocket she didn't understand, a coin inside a pouch inside a fear, and a list of names she could put to faces now: Lionel Hughes, Dr. Greta Morrison, Rita and Nolan, Betsy Kwon, Deena, Captain Reeves, the tall man with the hard jaw, the soft-spoken woman reading a battered book in 17A, Tamsin Roth. Mrs. Carmichael, silver hair swept back, hands folded on a canvas tote like a catechism.

When she reached the galley, she took one breath and counted to four, then let it go. That counted for prayer in an aircraft at night.

She lifted the kettle. She set cups in a line. She checked the time again, a habit as old as her first year on the line. She pressed her left pocket with two fingers. Paper there, not a comfort, but a weight that gave shape to the unknown.

"Everything all right?" Deena asked.

"For the moment," Amelia said.

"Hold that thought," Deena said.

Amelia held it for as long as the moment allowed.

CHAPTER TWO

Chapter 2

Amelia locked the cart at the forward galley and took a slow count of the cabin. Low light. A bead of condensation tracing down a plastic cup left on an armrest. Screen glow on faces. The air held the crush of a night flight when the first wave of jitters gave way to the second wave of thoughts no one invited.

Lionel's seat sat empty again. 23D. Belt slack. She checked the nearest lav. Occupied. She checked the aft. Also busy. Behind the curtain near first, a shape shifted like a watcher in a chapel aisle, the fabric breathing in and out with someone's faint movement.

She moved her hand over her left pocket, felt the rasp of torn edges under the lining. The two scraps rode there: *old score* and *the token*. Paper had weight beyond grams when it carried a message that sounded like a dare.

Seat checks next. She swept a row with her eyes and saw it: a single leather glove half tucked under Lionel's seat, right hand, worn smooth at the heel. She bent and took it in her palm. Inside the cuff: A.H., neat and precise, a stitcher's pride. She slid the glove beside the scraps in her left pocket and closed her hand against the seam. Left pocket now held a small archive, and every piece told her to wait, to not jump to an answer that might take her into a story she couldn't unmake.

Bradley Gaines in 20E pressed his call button with the resolve of a man who liked to win. "Is this delay going to cost me the meeting?" he asked.

"We're on schedule," Amelia said.

"On schedule for what?" he asked. "Another circle over the ocean?"

"On schedule for Paris," she said.

He snorted. Not loud. Enough to share his mood with the row.

Dr. Greta Morrison lifted a hand without impatience. "Blanket, if you've got one."

Amelia brought two, one for Greta and one for the woman in 12A who slept without one and would wake with a chill no one deserved.

Rita and Nolan had their heads together, a quiet bark of a couple squabble that measured more like love than friction. "It's not about the window," Rita said.

"It already wasn't about the window," Nolan said.

"Good," Rita said, and took his hand and threaded their fingers together until the small twitch in her jaw eased.

Near the first-class curtain, a whisper ran through like a wire pulled taut and then plucked. Amelia caught words, not a voice she could pin to any throat. "That token." Then, softer, the kind of promise that people made when they no longer cared what conscience thought: "Blood will be paid."

She held still. The curtain lay flat again. In that moment, the aircraft felt like a long corridor with every door closed, and somewhere in the corridor a footstep waited to be placed.

A photo skittered in the aisle as a passenger stood. She reached it before a shoe could crush it. A group of young people, coats and hair from another decade, stood shoulder to shoulder. At the far right, a face that carried the lines she had seen in Lionel's profile, a resemblance that hummed along the edge of her mind. A coffee ring marked the bottom corner. A deep crease ran across the faces like the fold of a letter read too many times. The owner of the photo, red-cheeked and breathless, snatched it back with a shake of the head.

"Drop something?" Amelia asked.

"Nothing," the passenger said, and turned the picture upside down as if that changed the truth of it.

She let it go. She put the date and the crease in the same mental column as the initials in the glove. If she wrote it all on actual paper, the page would look like a web.

Lionel returned to his row. He walked like a man who'd measured the distance to the lav and back in a different mood and hadn't found courage there. He had the velvet pouch cupped in his hand. He slid into 23D and set the pouch in his coat. One glove, left hand, in place. The right was missing from his pair. The match sat warm against her thigh in the left pocket.

She brought a bottle of water. "For you," she said.

"Thank you," he said. His voice scratched the air. He didn't look up right away. Then he did. "Forgive me," he said. "If I'm poor company tonight."

"You're fine," she said. "These nights are long."

He looked at her left hand, then at her face. "Be careful," he said. "People are not who they seem."

"That true in your row," she said, "or in every row?"

"In every row," he said. His fingers tightened on the bottle cap. The cap slipped. The bottle tilted. He caught it. The pouch in his coat shifted and thumped once against his ribs, a soft sound he seemed to hear more than feel.

"Call if you need anything," she said.

He nodded, then cooled his face with the damp of the bottle and stared straight ahead at a screen he didn't turn on.

She stepped back, gave the row air, and let her eye pass over 24C. A shadow in that seat. A chin. The rim of a cap. Nothing that would stand at a lineup later. She wrote the number again in her head, underlined it.

Rows farther forward calmed. A baby had found thumb and sleep at the same time. The older man in 9F read a small blue book with a gold cross and moved his lips to words he knew by heart. Mrs. Carmichael dozed with her tote against her knees and a little knit blanket across her hands.

The curtain near first twitched, just a touch. Lights flickered then steadied, a blink that might have been a breaker reset or a plane reminding them that even machines had moods. Amelia logged the time, because times mattered when stories broke later. The coin inside Lionel's coat had weight. The glove in her pocket had weight. Words on paper weighed nothing until they did.

Betsy drifted up with a cup and a smile. "Please tell me Paris invented a way to make time slower and also faster."

"It invented pastry," Amelia said.

"Close enough," Betsy said. "I heard the curtain sing. Did you hear words behind it?"

"Enough," Amelia said.

Betsy's eyes sharpened. "Enough to worry?"

"Enough to watch," Amelia said.

"I watch for sport," Betsy said. "I can make it service."

"Thank you," Amelia said. She meant it.

She moved past Greta and set a second blanket in her lap. Greta's fingers brushed the wool and then stayed there like the fabric kept her in one piece. "History doesn't sleep," Greta said, not to Amelia, not to anyone else, just to the air, then went quiet.

At 17A, Tamsin Roth read her worn book with a stillness that had edge, the kind of stillness people used when they trained themselves to not react. Her eyes tracked in a way that said she read to the end of lines and looked past them at something only she could see. When Amelia passed, Tamsin's fingers closed around the book a shade tighter, and then loosened as if she remembered that a closed fist made people ask questions.

Amelia reached the galley and poured coffee for a pilot break that might come at any moment or not at all. She checked the panel that tracked lav use. She entered a quiet note on a pad: Lionel's seat vacant at these times. Not an accusation. A map.

"Tea for me," Rita said, appearing like a whisper. "With honey if you have it."

"I have it," Amelia said.

Nolan peered around the corner, grin back in place like it hadn't left. "We're making a schedule for sleep. It's a terrible plan."

"They always are," Amelia said, and handed him a cup of water he hadn't asked for but would need.

On her way back, she caught sight of a photo corner peeking out of Lionel's coat, a nicked edge that matched the coffee-ringed print she'd picked up. If she named the feeling that rose in her, she'd call it the click a key made when it turned in a lock that had waited for the right hand.

He stood, then sat, then stood again. She let him. Sometimes movement drained off charge you couldn't set down.

Lights flickered a second time, a blink only a few would log, but the few mattered. The curtain stirred. From somewhere near 24C came a line spoken as if the speaker carried it from another room in another year. "It never ended," the voice said. "And it will not end now."

Amelia looked up, and in the thin second before quiet returned, all the threads in her left pocket tugged at once.

CHAPTER THREE

Chapter 3

The cabin rested in a hush that belonged to high sky. Plastic cups nested in a tidy stack on the cart. A thin line of frost traced the window at 14F where a man leaned his head and slept with his mouth open. Amelia moved through the aisle with the steady gait that kept her weight centered. Screens cast a blue wash on hands and cheeks. A napkin on a tray curled at one corner and stayed that way, a small flag against a current no one named.

Lionel sat upright in 23D with a pocket notebook balanced on his knee. The cover had a ring mark, a circle left by some old drink. He wrote in quick bursts, the pencil making a soft scratch. He used his left hand. His left hand still wore the glove that matched the one in Amelia's pocket. He paused, tapped the pencil on the page once, then wrote again. The velvet pouch pressed against his ribs inside his coat as if he had sewn it there.

Amelia collected two empty cups from row twenty-one. A girl in 20C slept with her head on her mother's shoulder. Betsy rolled the aft cart to a stop and breathed through her nose like a sprinter who had learned patience.

Greta stood from 22A and stepped to the aisle with a look that said this would not be a short exchange. She stopped beside Lionel. "There's a ledger behind that coin," she said. "A history that would make a museum's board lean forward. There's a long-lost fortune at stake."

Lionel closed the notebook and slid it into his coat. "Find another subject," he said.

"I think you carry the final piece," Greta said. "Please hear me. The families will not stop."

"I said no," he said.

Greta held his gaze a beat. Then she stepped back. She took her blanket with her and sat, eyes on the pouch line under his coat.

Captain Reeves pinged the belt sign from the flight deck. "Ladies and gentlemen," his voice came through the cabin speaker. "We've got some rough air ahead. Please return to your seats and fasten seat belts."

Seat belts clicked. Amelia moved the cart to a galley lock and latched it. Betsy caught Amelia's eye and smiled in the wry way that drew a grin out of people who thought they didn't have one. "I wanted a quiet crossword," she said. "This flight keeps tossing letters at me."

"You'll solve it," Amelia said.

"Not if the letters jump," Betsy said.

The aircraft rolled and rose, a long heave that set a fork on 19D to chime against its plate. A ripple of breath traveled the rows, the collective sound of people choosing to trust metal and crew and a pilot they did not meet. Amelia checked her left pocket for the two scraps of paper and the right-hand glove. Paper rasped against her finger, a small grit that kept her anchored to purpose.

Lights dimmed, then steadied, then dimmed farther. The belt sign glowed with a stern red face. A tray slid a hand's width and stopped against a cup. Amelia braced one palm at a seatback, kept her weight low, and scanned for loose baggage.

The lights flicked and cut. Night took the cabin in one clean throw. A boy gasped. Someone whispered a prayer. In the dark, a voice near row twenty-three rang along the aisle, hard with shock. "What are you doing?!"

A thud. Not heavy. Close. Amelia's chest went tight. She counted to three and felt for the flashlight on her belt.

Light returned in a wave of return power, then held, a pale wash that set faces in stark relief. Lionel slumped over his tray, head turned to the side, throat pushing a thin breath. His notebook had slid half out of his coat. The velvet pouch line no longer showed under the fabric.

"Call for a doctor," Amelia said to Betsy.

"I'm on it," Betsy said, already raising a hand. "Is anyone a physician?"

A man in row ten half stood and lifted his card from his wallet as if he had written M.D. on it in large block letters for moments like this. "Yes," he said. He came forward with a measured step. "What happened?"

"Blackout," Amelia said. "He spoke. Then something hit."

The physician checked Lionel's wrist, then his neck. "Pulse faint," he said. "Breathing shallow but regular." He lifted Lionel's eyelid and watched the pupil. "We need him supine."

"Help me move him," Amelia said.

They cleared the tray, lowered the seatback, and slid Lionel into a safer angle. The physician fitted a portable oxygen line from the kit. Lionel's chest rose and fell with the soft push of oxygen.

Greta stood at the aisle edge with her hands clamped at her sides, eyes flat as stone. "I'm a doctor," she said. "But not medical."

"Then give us space," the physician said.

Deena arrived with the AED and a packet of wipes. "Tell me we don't need this," she said.

"Not yet," the physician said. "He's perfusing. Keep me the oxygen."

Amelia slid a hand into Lionel's coat. The pouch was gone. The pocket turned inside out near a loose thread.

She checked the seat pocket, the floor under his shoes, the gap between seat and wall. Nothing that glinted. Nothing with weight.

"Where's the coin?" Greta asked.

"It's not on him," Amelia said.

A woman across the aisle put a hand to her mouth. "He cried out," she said. "Then a shape leaned in."

"What did you see?" Amelia asked.

"Tall," the woman said. "A long coat. Could have been a man. Could have been a woman with a square build." She shook her head once, as if to clear fog. "The lights died. I can't swear."

From behind, a man in 24D leaned over his armrest. "I saw someone move from 24C," he said. "Fast. A reach, then a shove."

Amelia wrote the number in her head again. 24C. The enigma seat. She looked. A head bent over a book. A cap brim. The angle made a shield of shadow.

"Sit back," Amelia said to both rows, voice calm. "We'll canvas in a moment."

The aircraft hit a fresh pocket and bounced. Overhead bins rattled with a long, shaken shiver. An oxygen mask door in row twenty popped open and banged, a plastic clack that drew three gasps and one small cry. The masks did not fall. The door hung there, a bright yellow lid at a wrong angle.

Betsy reached to snap it shut. The latch refused. She eased it back into place and let it rest.

"Captain," Amelia said into the interphone. "We had a full loss for a breath. Passenger down with stable pulse. Oxygen door popped on row twenty."

"Understood," Captain Reeves said. "Rough patch. Systems are holding. We'll ride it out."

Passengers watched Amelia and read their own safety from her face. That came with the job. She smoothed her expression into one that turned down panic and turned up trust. The physician checked Lionel's pulse again and gave a short nod.

Greta drew close. "He kept a notebook," she said. "I saw it."

Amelia pulled the small book from under Lionel's coat and handed it to the physician first. He checked for clear medical info, then shook his head and passed it back. Amelia tucked it into her left pocket with the scraps and the glove. The pocket held a growing story.

"Do you see any medication?" the physician asked.

"No," Amelia said.

Betsy stood hip to seat with her back set as a shield. "He said 'what are you doing,'" she said, voice low so it would not travel. "That wasn't for show. Someone reached him."

"We'll check every angle," Amelia said.

Row twenty-three gave the soft push of bodies trying not to stare and failing. Amelia understood. People leaned toward trouble because it proved they were alive.

She crouched and swept her hand along the floor edge. Dust, a pen cap, the corner of a candy wrapper. No coin. The velvet pouch had left no trace.

Greta breathed through her nose and stared at Lionel. "That coin draws hands," she said. "It always has."

"What do you mean, always?" Amelia asked.

Greta blinked once as if she had stepped off a curb she thought was a step. "Ignore me," she said. "I speak in habits."

"Don't," Amelia said. "Habits matter."

Another bump rolled through the airframe. Not big. Enough to lift a few stomachs. A baby startled and then sighed. Cups rattled. The belt sign stayed lit.

The physician adjusted the oxygen flow. Lionel made a sound, a whisper that did not climb to a word. His brow knit. His hand twitched at his side. Then he lay still again, breathing with the soft hiss of the mask.

"Keep him here for now," the physician said. "Aft would be better for monitoring when seats open."

"I'll clear a space," Amelia said.

She moved to the galley and keyed the interphone to Captain Reeves. "We need a calm update for the cabin," she said. "One sentence about rough air. Assure them the flight deck has it in hand."

"Done," he said.

His voice carried into the cabin with that even tone that could sell water to fish. Passengers settled a degree.

Amelia returned to row twenty-three and began the quick canvass. "If you were awake during the lights out," she said, "I need what you heard and where you looked. Keep to what you can stand by."

A man in 22D raised a finger. "Someone stood from 24C," he said. "But I can't swear they leaned across. They could have gone to the lav if they changed their mind when the light died."

"Thank you," Amelia said.

A woman in 23A shook her head. "I heard a sleeve brush a seat," she said. "Could have been anyone."

"Thank you," Amelia said again.

An older passenger three rows back gave a small cough. Mrs. Carmichael. She had her tote clutched tight to her chest. "I saw a hand," she said. "Wide. Square knuckles."

"That narrows some," Amelia said.

"Or I imagine it," Mrs. Carmichael said, voice thinner than an hour ago.

"We'll build the picture," Amelia said.

She logged 24C again. The curtain near first stirred with a touch of air and settled. The popped oxygen door in row twenty hung at a slant like a sign no one read yet.

Deena returned with a seat freed in the aft row near the galley. Together they eased Lionel back, the physician steady at his shoulder. The plane took another shake during the move. Amelia braced and set her foot in a way that made her a wall for two seconds. Then it passed. They set Lionel in the last row where the physician could watch him without fielding too many questions.

Amelia turned back through the aisle. Greta stayed in her seat and folded her hands as if in prayer. Betsy stood guard near 24C with the casual stance of a woman watching a kettle that might boil over.

"Everything under control?" Rita asked from 18B. Her hand had found Nolan's again.

"We're on top of it," Amelia said. "Seat belts, please."

Nolan touched his buckle and clicked it into place as if the buckle could be courage.

Amelia checked the floor again at 23D. She looked under the bag at his feet, under the tray hinge, along the edge where grit gathered.

The coin did not want to be found. It hid somewhere in a pocket, a palm, a mind that had waited for dark.

She straightened and checked the oxygen door that refused to latch. It hung in quiet threat, the kind of thing that moved people from ask to shout if it fell.

"Leave it for now," the physician called from the back. "Focus on people."

Amelia looked at the page in her mind where she kept all moving parts. On that page, she underlined three lines: coin missing; blackout voice; 24C shadow. She pressed a thumb to her left pocket and felt the edges of paper cut across the glove fur. The pocket gave back a cold that meant attention.

She met Betsy's eyes. Betsy lifted her chin a fraction toward 24C.

"Later," Amelia mouthed.

Betsy gave a small nod.

The aircraft smoothed a fraction. The belt sign still glowed. Lights held to low. The door in row twenty kept its wrong angle and waited, as if the cabin had not had its fill. The night outside stayed blank, an ocean of nothing with a city a world ahead.

CHAPTER FOUR

Chapter 4

After the rough air passed, the cabin settled into a fragile balance. People measured their breaths. Amelia radioed forward and received a short update from Captain Reeves for the speaker. He told the cabin the bump was behind them while systems stayed steady. Then he turned the sign off for a few minutes to let a few people move, before he lit it again as a reminder that the night liked surprises.

With Deena and the physician, Amelia eased Lionel into the last row by the aft galley where the doctor could watch his chest rise without blocking the aisle. The man's face had a gray cast that belonged to fever dreams. The oxygen line fed him a thin promise. The coin still did not show. She made a neat pass through 23D's space and the floor again, then called it and logged the missing item.

Opinions grew legs. In the row behind Lionel's, a man pointed to his own chest and said, "Looks like a heart hit to me. Panic. Altitude. These things happen."

A woman across from him shook her head. "He cried out," she said. "Someone touched him. You heard it."

"Keep your voices low," Amelia said. "We're helping him. The physician has him stable. We'll track everything else."

Greta waited at her seat with the posture of a lecturer who had asked to speak and been told to hold. When Amelia came near, Greta lifted a hand. "I have context," she said.

"I'm listening," Amelia said.

"The coin marks a claim," Greta said. "A line out of France, older than a few modern countries on the map. de Riviere. The crest on that coin sets position at a long table where estates and debts get counted. Return that coin to one branch, you settle an old line. Sell it to the wrong hands, you spark a war in a house that thinks it runs the world." She paused. "I am not here to buy it. I want it cataloged and archived."

"Did you tell Lionel that?" Amelia asked.

"I told him to stop running," Greta said. "He told me to stop speaking."

"Then we're in the same choir," Amelia said.

Betsy sidled up, eyes bright with information she did not trust but could not leave alone. "I keep my ears open," she said. "Near row fifteen a woman wore a cameo brooch with a crest that looked like the coin. Same shield, same crown above. I heard the words unpaid debt in the washroom line. Not a guess."

"Who wore the brooch?" Amelia asked.

"I can draw the shape of her hair," Betsy said. "The face is fuzz in my head. These lights do favors and then take them back."

"We'll look for it," Amelia said.

Bradley Gaines in 20E chose that moment to launch a solo show. "How long will this take?" he asked, voice pitched to hit five rows. "I have a time-locked meeting. This man and his drama just cost me a contract."

"Sir, sit back," Amelia said. "We're working. We'll bring water once the aisle clears."

"I don't want water," Bradley said. "I want arrival. This is a plane, not a stage."

"We hear you," Amelia said. "Seat belt, please."

Bradley glared, then buckled. He looked past Amelia as if he could burn a hole through a bulkhead with will alone.

With permission from the physician and a nod from Captain Reeves, Amelia opened Lionel's carry-on to look for medical bracelets, allergies, anything that could help. She found a wallet with a faded membership card to an antiques club, a pen case, and a flat folder wrapped in string. Inside, a single photograph: Lionel younger by a decade, standing next to a stern older man in a dark coat whose jaw could break glass. A second item bore a neat label on the flap: Paris, 1982. The envelope paper felt thicker than modern make, a stock that promised the weight of old quarrels.

She did not break the seal. That would need consent or cause. She logged both items and set them back.

"Anything there?" Deena asked.

"History," Amelia said. "Answers later."

She moved up the aisle for a quick cross-check. People gave her small slices of words.

"I saw a figure, tall, in the aisle," one said.

"Nothing," said another. "I had my eyes shut when the light died."

"A coat sleeve at Lionel's elbow," said a third. "Could have been anyone."

"Did you see who sits in 24C?" Amelia asked a man two rows behind.

He shook his head. "Hat. Head down. That's all."

"Thank you," she said.

She passed row fifteen and saw a brooch on a soft cardigan, a cameo set in silver with a crest so small it read as a blur. The woman's hair had been pinned back in a twist. Betsy's memory served. Amelia bent and smiled. "Lovely piece," she said.

"Gift," the woman said.

"Special crest," Amelia said.

The woman fingered the brooch. "Family," she said, and let the word fall with a weight it had earned.

Amelia carried that weight back toward Greta. "You win a point," she said.

"I did not want the point," Greta said.

Rita raised a hand as Amelia passed. "He's going to live, right?" she asked.

"He has a pulse and oxygen," Amelia said. "The doctor's with him. We'll land with him breathing."

Nolan squeezed Rita's hand and held her eyes until she smiled. It worked, a small magic that people passed between them when the night pressed.

Amelia returned to the aft row to check Lionel and speak to the physician. "If we need to divert," she said, "how much time do you need for a stronger call?"

"He holds now," the physician said. "If his rhythm slides or his airway changes, I'll tell you. For now we watch."

"Thank you," she said.

She checked the panel above row twenty. The oxygen door that had popped sat flush now. Some latches healed when shaken. Others broke for good. She logged the seat number and moved on.

At mid-cabin, Bradley stood again and spread his arms as if he had bought the aisle with his ticket. "So we do nothing?" he asked.

"We keep the aisle clear," Amelia said. "We serve what we can. We keep the cabin calm."

"Calm," Bradley said, as if it were a foolish word. He sat. He shook his head. He tapped his knee. He carved the air once with his hand and stopped when three people looked at him the way you looked at noise in a library.

Greta rose and stepped into the galley where Amelia stood. "There's a name you need," she said, softer now. "de Riviere. That's the crest. If the coin and any partner piece return to a museum, you end this. If they move through private hands, a dozen claims wake."

"Partner piece," Amelia said. "What kind of partner?"

"A locket," Greta said. "A cameo. I think someone speaks about it already."

"Betsy heard that too," Amelia said.

Greta touched her head where a bruise would later show under hair. "I have an item that matches the era," she said. "Not the coin."

"Show me," Amelia said.

"In a moment," Greta said. "I want to watch him breathe for one minute more."

Amelia brought water to three rows, then paused at 24C and let her eyes move in a slow arc that counted items without staring. A book jacket with a torn corner. A cap brim. A coat folded with care. A hand tucked under a thigh. The figure did not look up. She noted the quiet, then continued.

Betsy sidled up again with the look of a friend who had brought a rumor to the back door. "I heard two men whisper about unpaid debt," she said. "It came from near row twelve. Or nine. Lights play tricks on distance."

"Who said the words?" Amelia asked.

"Hard to pin," Betsy said. "One had a low voice that tried to hide its own shape."

"We'll run it as a line," Amelia said.

She finished a water pass, then returned to Lionel's bag with the physician's nod. "Do you mind if I pull any medical detail from his wallet?" she asked.

"Do it," the physician said. "He can consent later."

She looked again through basic cards. No allergies. No meds. She glanced at the 1982 envelope again and put it back where it lay. Some doors you did not open in midair without a key.

She found Lionel's phone and brought it to the doctor. "If we can unlock this," she said, "we might find a health record."

"Later," he said. "Pulse first."

The cabin rode another small tremor, then went still. Captain Reeves gave them another reassurance from the flight deck. People leaned back a notch.

"Am I the only one who thinks poison," a man in 21C whispered to his row mate.

"Could be a heart," the row mate whispered back. "My uncle dropped at a wedding and came back after cake."

"You two," Amelia said, gentle but firm. "Keep it kind. Words travel."

They nodded like boys caught throwing pebbles at a pond.

A minute later Amelia caught sight of a thin silver line at the lip of Greta's jacket pocket. It flashed then tucked away like a fish stripe under a wave. She lifted her chin toward it.

Greta placed a hand over the pocket. "A spoon," she said. "From a set I study. Silver before the Revolution. It has the crest."

"May I see it?" Amelia asked.

"In a second," Greta said. "Not here."

Amelia nodded. She kept a neutral face and a careful breath. The silver had weight as a clue even if it turned out to be a fork, a pin, a piece of an old set that proved nothing. The coin stayed gone. The cabin fed on rumor and grew new branches for the story with each new whisper.

Captain Reeves stepped out just enough to look down the aisle, then vanished back into the sealed room where calm lived on checklists. Amelia watched the cabin pulse and settle. She checked her left pocket again. Paper edges pressed against the glove fur. The scrap with the words old score had softened with body heat but stayed legible. The matching scrap with the word token pushed back against her knuckle.

She made one more pass for witness lines. "During the black-out," she said to the man who had claimed the tall figure, "do you recall a scent or a sound besides the voice?"

"A coat swish," he said. "Like wool. No cologne. A shoe scraped once."

"Thank you," she said.

At 24C the figure turned a page and kept the brim down. The brim could be a shield or a habit. She logged the posture, the page turns, the quiet.

By the time she reached the galley, Greta stood with her jacket closed again and her mouth set.

"Show me the spoon," Amelia said.

Greta slipped a silver utensil from her pocket just far enough for the crest to catch light. A shield, a crown, a small river line cut across the base like an artist's joke. Then she hid it again. "Not a theft," she said. "A study object for a paper."

"Understood," Amelia said. "Keep it put away for now."

Greta nodded. "My work involves walls and labels," she said. "Not aisles."

"None of us planned this," Amelia said.

A chime sounded from the flight deck. Captain Reeves told the cabin that the ride looked smooth ahead. A breath went out of a dozen chests at once. Amelia let her own shoulders loosen a hair. She looked down the aisle toward 23D where Lionel now lay under the eyes of the physician and the green edge of the oxygen line.

The coin did not show. The spoon's glint sat where a coin could have glinted. The cabin chose its suspects with light and rumor and the old shape of people's fear. Amelia turned toward 24C, ready to make another pass.

CHAPTER FIVE

Chapter 5

The lights along the ceiling softened to a sleepy glow, and the night outside pressed its cold face to the windows. The air carried coffee, fabric softener, and the faint mineral scent of the sealed sky. The engine hum housed a rhythm that steadied nerves and hid secrets.

Amelia set a cup on a saucer in the forward galley and watched the steam rise. She wrapped the tea bag in twine over the handle so the tag wouldn't slip and stain. A simple cup, the oldest truce in the world. She carried it down the aisle.

Greta sat half turned toward the window, a pale oval of face above a dark collar. Her hands, resting on a manila folder, shook in tiny pulses that didn't fit her controlled posture.

"Tea," Amelia said.

Greta's mouth tipped in thanks. "You're kind." She lifted the cup, and the surface trembled. "No sugar."

Amelia let a beat pass.

"The coin," Greta said. "Everyone keeps whispering about it."

"The coin has made people nervous," Amelia said.

A flash tightened Greta's jaw. "I study objects like that. I do not pocket them."

"I didn't say you did."

"You didn't have to."

Amelia kept her voice even. "People on night flights spin stories. I try to keep them from spinning out."

Greta breathed in the steam. "I'm a historian. I'm here on a research program. You can verify that."

"I will." Amelia nodded. "The lights will dim for a technical check, just a small adjustment from the flight deck. If you need anything during that, press your call light."

Greta sipped. Her hand stayed unsteady. The folder on her knee slid a finger's width. Paper edges showed.

The cabin lights faded one degree more. A few screens went black then returned. In the near hush, a zipper rasped, a sigh traveled a row and stopped.

Greta shifted, and the folder tilted. Pages fanned across the seat and the carpet. Photographs, copies, a gray print of a family crest, an old portrait, a sheet with ink in tidy lines. Amelia crouched and lifted the top photo: a stern-faced man in a stiff collar posed near a stone balustrade. His eyes, intense even across a century, looked like a harder version of Lionel's.

"Careful," Greta said. She reached for the pages with a quick little grab. "Please."

Amelia passed the photo back. A corner of a typed page stuck to her wrist. She eased it loose. A sentence ran bold in the middle of the page, as if brave ink could stop a century of trouble: *last rightful heir must protect it at all costs.*

Greta snatched the sheet, folded it into the file, and pressed the folder shut.

"Who wrote that?" Amelia asked.

"A curator who loved drama," Greta said. "You know the type."

"Someone wrote it with purpose."

Greta set the cup on the armrest and tried for calm. "Purpose is not proof. You should keep your crew safe. Let us handle the rest once we land."

"Us?"

"My museum partners."

Amelia studied the tremor that refused to leave Greta's fingers. The tremor didn't look like guilt. It looked like fear dressed in silk and Latin footnotes.

A chime popped. The captain's voice floated out, steady as a man holding the yoke with two clean hands. "Cabin crew, we are running a brief systems check. Lights will remain low for a few minutes. No cause for concern."

In row 18, Rita tugged Nolan's sleeve.

"Bad?" Rita asked.

Nolan shook his head. "Checks are good. Checks keep us up here."

Betsy raised a cup from across the aisle. "To checks," she said.

Amelia stood. "I'll be in the galley for a minute," she told Greta.

Greta gave a small nod and stared at the sealed night.

Amelia reached the galley and tapped the interphone. "Purser, I need a quick look at a booking."

The purser came off a manifest like a priest with a liturgy. "Name?"

"Dr. Greta Morrison. Booked under a research program."

Keys clicked. Paper slid. The answer came with a careful pause. "The booking shows an academic fare class and a notation for research. Not a full verification from any institution."

"Copy," Amelia said. "Thanks."

A gust of laughter drifted from the honeymooners' row, then hushed itself, as if laughter worried about drawing attention. Deena passed with a trash bag and a long look. "You and your clues," she said in a low voice. "You collect them like souvenir spoons."

"They keep collecting me," Amelia said.

"Just don't fall in," Deena said, and angled away.

Amelia moved back to Greta's seat. The historian's folder lay shut again, but a corner of an envelope peeked from the side. The paper looked stiff, older than the copy stock. Greta rose a little.

"I should stretch," Greta said. "Lavatory?"

"Of course," Amelia said.

Greta stood and stepped into the aisle. She kept the folder pressed against her ribs, not clutching, not casual, a narrow space between those two poles where fear learns to walk. She moved toward the forward lav, then hesitated, then veered behind the business-class curtain.

Betsy materialized near Amelia's shoulder like a friendly ghost. She thumbed at the empty seat. "She left that envelope half tucked. I saw a phrase."

"What phrase?"

Betsy lifted an eyebrow. "You'll scold me."

"Try me."

"*Last rightful heir must protect it at all costs.*"

Amelia kept her face still.

Betsy leaned in. "You know I don't lie. I do hear wrong sometimes. But I read that clean."

"Thank you," Amelia said.

She gave the seat a quick, neat glance. The envelope had gone with Greta. A tiny sliver of copy paper remained under the armrest, like a white tongue stuck between teeth. Amelia let it be. Chain of custody. She turned toward the curtain.

The lights dipped again. An older man cleared his throat. Somewhere, a child asked for water. A call light winked above row 24, lingered, then went dark.

Deena swished back, eyes scanning. "She cut through the business galley," Deena murmured. "I heard two voices back there, soft. Then nothing."

"Describe the other voice," Amelia said.

"Hard to place," Deena said. "Not loud. Not Lionel."

Amelia parted the curtain. The galley beyond held stainless faces and folded linens and the smell of onions trapped in cool metal. No one stood there. The aft curtain lifted and fell in a mild breath the plane makes for itself when it can, the little sigh that passes down the spine of the fuselage.

She checked the lav. Empty.

She stepped back into the cabin.

Rita rubbed her forearms. "Someone keeps staring," she said.

"Where?" Amelia asked.

"Not one place," Rita said. "Like the feeling you get in a museum when the eyes on a painting follow you around the room."

Nolan squeezed her hand. "I'll swap seats if it helps."

"Stay together," Amelia said. "We'll be at cruise for a while. No heavy bumps on the schedule."

Bradley grunted in row 20. "Schedule," he said. "Tell that to the client who thinks the world runs on punctual miracles."

"Sir," Amelia said. "We'll do everything we can."

He raised his hands in a little show of innocence. "I'm not the one passing secret notes."

Amelia moved on. She kept scanning for a scarf or a corner of a folder or a shoe angled wrong.

A chime pinged. The seat belt sign lit. The captain again: "Seat belts for a brief patch of unsettled air."

Amelia took a breath that tasted like coffee and aluminum and something like dust from old paper. The plane steadied. The lights remained low.

Greta's seat stayed empty.

Amelia crossed to the purser station and kept her voice level. "We have a passenger out of sight," she said. "Booked under a research program. She headed toward the business galley and did not return."

"Report it," the purser said.

"Let's keep it quiet for now," Amelia said. "No panic. People will fill the void with stories."

"Stories are already in the aisles," the purser said.

Amelia glanced at the clock near the forward bulkhead. She logged the minute. She wrote a neat note on a thin card in her pocket: Greta last seen, business galley, dim lights, seat belt on.

A blanket slid off a lap and folded itself on the floor. A passenger snored once then stopped, as if embarrassed by his own noise. A phone, set to airplane mode, glowed with a picture of two children in matching pajamas.

Amelia moved curtain to curtain, eyes open to corners, then turned toward the front. She lifted the curtain into the narrow corridor near the cockpit door. The floor there carried a different grip underfoot, a patch of textured rubber made for boots and purpose. The light changed by a shade she knew from years of service, that pale tone near a lock.

No one waited in the corridor. No one should.

She went back to the cabin. Deena came fast from aft, a strip of color clutched in her hand. The strip fluttered like a wounded flag.

"Amelia," Deena said. "Her scarf. Near the cockpit door."

They moved together to the small space again. Deena lifted the scarf. The weave was fine, a light gray with a stitched crest near the end. The crest matched the one on Greta's folder pages. At the scarf's tip, a single dot bloomed, rust red against the thread.

Amelia stood very still and listened to the hum have its say. The engine's steady music told her this: the night wanted a cost.

She folded the scarf across her palm without touching the stain.

"We'll keep the cabin calm," she said.

Deena nodded, mouth set.

Amelia looked down the aisle at the empty seat where a cup of tea cooled on a folding arm. The steam had left. The ring it would make on the plastic would dry to a faint circle, a ghost mark that would say, someone was here, and then the sky asked for her.

"Seat belts," the captain said. "Everyone remain seated."

Amelia lifted her head and moved.

The cabin watched the crew with a hundred sets of eyes. She met them all with the single message people trust more than any speech: I am at work, and I will not stop.

She did not stop.

Chapter 6

The cabin carried small sounds: ice settling in a drawer, a zipper tooth clicking, the low chorus of air over metal. Somewhere, someone whispered grace before sleep. The lights stayed soft, like stars behind thin cloud.

Amelia and Deena split the plane on an invisible line. A sweep, but not one that would break nerves. Deena took aft with slow steps and a trash bag that said everything was fine. Amelia took forward, her hands empty to show she held no panic.

She checked the forward lav, then the mid. She checked under a jumpseat for a fallen scarf, a pen, a note. She checked the narrow spaces by the galley carts. She made eye contact with people who needed it. The message did not change: We see you. You're safe.

Captain Reeves met her at the interphone. His eyes had the steady patience that kept metal honest. "Keep it quiet," he said. "We have a systems check, but we're stable. I'll handle any announcements."

"We'll find her," Amelia said.

He gave a single nod and disappeared into the flight deck, a door that accepted no theater.

Near the rear of economy, the traveling physician rose partway. "How's our patient?" Amelia asked.

"Steady. As steady as this allows," he said. He tapped Lionel's IV line with a gentle finger. "We wait and guard."

Amelia crossed to Lionel. His skin held the gray of someone who lost a race and still reaches for the ribbon. The forearm bruise had spread to a small coin of shadow near a vein.

"Do you need water?" she asked.

His lips moved without sound. She leaned closer, careful not to touch tubes or tape.

"The claim," Lionel whispered. His breath scraped like paper. "Beware the false friend."

His eyes caught hers with a bright, helpless shine, then drifted past her shoulder to some ledger only he could read. The physician lowered a hand.

"Rest," Amelia said.

Lionel's mouth tried to form another word, then gave up. His hand stayed limp on the armrest, gloved on the left, bare on the right. The glove's embroidery caught the light and threw it back in a tiny spark.

Amelia straightened. The cabin looked the same as it had ten minutes before, which was the trick cabins pull when people go missing and a cup cools and a scarf waits by a locked door.

She went to meet Deena in the galley. Deena had her back to the coffee machine and her face bent near a gap where a panel met the counter. She held a stir stick, slid the stick into the gap, and drew it back with a tiny flake of something like brittle paper.

"What is it?" Amelia asked.

"A crumb," Deena said. "Not food."

Amelia bent and peered into the slim seam. A crease hid there, where no one would put anything on purpose. She took a butter knife and eased the panel a breath. A slip of aged paper sighed out and fell against her hand.

The paper had that dry weight old documents carry, like skin cured by time. Along the top edge ran a line of script in a thin, slanted hand. Amelia read aloud without meaning to. "Vow of silence."

Deena looked up. "We're not in church," she said.

"Feels like one," Amelia said.

She turned the paper in careful fingers. The ink faded at the edges of letters. A paragraph down, three words stood in a row like hoofprints across a field: *estate dispute continues*. A line lower: *token must never be relinquished*. The crest in the corner matched the one in Greta's folder, a looped river, a crown, a sword exact as a rule.

Betsy appeared with perfect timing and leaned on the door-frame. "I came for decaf," she said. "I'd settle for tea. I'd also settle for the story behind the faces you're making."

"Decaf," Amelia said.

"I heard three different versions of a feud from row 14 to 17," Betsy said. "One person asked if the coin could open a secret vault. Another thinks it's cursed. Another said it belongs in a drawer with loose screws and dead batteries."

Amelia poured and set the cup in Betsy's hands. "Drink."

Betsy sipped and nodded like a judge. "Good," she said. "No curse in that."

Amelia slid the old paper back into the gap and taped a note at the edge: HOLD FOR AUTHORITIES. Then she took a breath that didn't fill as completely as she liked.

"Let's keep moving," she told Deena.

They wove forward. Mrs. Carmichael lifted a small hand from a window seat and touched Amelia's sleeve with two fingers as if she reached across a fragile surface.

"I saw her," Mrs. Carmichael said.

"Where?" Amelia asked.

"The corridor near the cockpit," Mrs. Carmichael said. "She had her folder tucked in. She looked... set."

"Set how?"

"As if she'd made up her mind," Mrs. Carmichael said. Her voice thinned on the next words. "The name on that parchment. I knew that name once. I knew a man who said it like a prayer and like a threat. It can do both."

"Which name?" Amelia asked.

"De Riviere," Mrs. Carmichael said.

She drew the syllables out with a careful mouth and placed them between them like a small breakable thing.

"Did Greta speak to anyone there?" Amelia asked.

"A shadow leaned toward her," Mrs. Carmichael said. "Not tall. A shape more than a person. Then the corridor cleared. I thought she had gone back to her seat."

"She didn't," Amelia said.

Mrs. Carmichael's eyes filmed. "I knew a feuding family long ago," she said. "People carried grudges like heirlooms. You polish an heirloom. You feed a grudge, and it grows teeth."

Amelia kept her tone warm. "If you remember anything more, tell me."

Mrs. Carmichael nodded and bent toward the window again, where the black outside pressed its persistence on the glass.

Amelia walked on. A row up, Nolan whispered into Rita's hair. Rita's eyes tracked the aisle, the way a bird tracks for snakes without meaning to.

"We'll bring snack service again soon," Amelia said.

Rita nodded. "I'm fine," she said, which is the sentence people use when they're not.

The seat belt sign blinked off, then on again, a wink, then a reminder. Captain Reeves kept the cabin informed with steady beats, not too many, not too few.

Amelia checked the forward corridor again. The scarf waited by the door where Deena had left it folded on a service ledge, the crest visible, the red dot darker now, oxidizing into brown. She took a photo with the cabin phone's camera for the record and logged the time and location. She looked down the line where the door's hinges sat under paneling. Everything looked intact. No passenger should be here. No sound came from the other side of reinforced metal but the murmur of voices through comms.

"I'll alert the captain," she said to Deena.

Deena nodded. "Do it."

Amelia lifted the interphone and spoke to Reeves in a quiet, precise voice reserved for real things. When she hung up, she found her hand had closed tight around the pen. She eased her grip and flexed her fingers.

Betsy reached the row of the honeymooners and crouched, easy as a friend. "I can teach you a breathing trick," she told Rita. "Count the rivets near the window. It's fake math, but it fools your brain into calm."

Rita peered at the panel beside her seat. "There are a lot of rivets."

"Good," Betsy said. "Pick your ten favorites."

Rita smiled despite herself. Nolan shook his head and laughed once, then covered his mouth as if he'd broken a rule. The sound did the cabin good. Laughter has a way of nailing boards across a hole in the floor.

Amelia moved on.

At the bulkhead, the traveling physician checked his watch. He had the patient calm people get on long shifts in rooms with soft beeps.

"How's he doing?" Amelia asked.

"Stable," the physician said. "He tried to speak again. Nothing clean."

"He mentioned a false friend."

The physician's mouth set. "That tracks with the rest of tonight."

Greta still had not returned.

Amelia stepped into the business-class galley again and opened the trash flap. She scanned for a crumple of paper with notes, for a glove, for a strip of gray thread. Nothing jumped. She checked the small drawer where the safety cards sometimes snag. Nothing. She checked the floor under the cart's lowest shelf and found a coin of sticky soda where a cup had tipped in some earlier hour. She wiped it clean.

She remembered her father once under a streetlamp with rain graining the glow and the ground slick with oil rainbows. He'd told her people hide the worst of their intentions in plain sight when folks grow tired. "That's when you look twice," he'd said. "Tired eyes skip."

Her eyes did not skip.

She returned to economy to check the overhead bins near rows 23 and 24, where a rumor earlier had caught like lint on a sweater. She lifted the latch and eased it down. No one had stashed a new bag. She closed the bin and recorded the check with a neat mark.

Mrs. Carmichael raised her hand again. "I'm sorry," she said. "One more thing. The parchment you held. I knew a clerk in Lyon who made copies from an old book with that crest. The clerk told me the family had a rule. They passed it from dying mouth to next ear. It spoke of silence more than justice."

"Thank you," Amelia said.

Mrs. Carmichael's voice thinned. "Silence does not fix anything. It just keeps pain warm for the next generation."

The cabin creaked a little under a change in pressure like a ship in a cold current. The plane held true.

Deena jogged up with her stride grown short and tight. She had the scarf in a clear evidence sleeve now, the crest visible, the stain like a drop of punctuation at the end of a sentence no one wanted to finish.

"Found right by the door," Deena said. "I did a second pass along the corridor before I bagged it. Nothing else."

"Good," Amelia said. "We'll log it with the captain."

Rita saw the sleeve and hugged herself. Nolan put his arm around her shoulders and pulled her in.

Bradley spoke over the seatback from two rows behind them. "So now we're collecting fashion accessories as evidence. Wonderful."

Amelia kept her tone measured. "Sir, please remain seated."

"Gladly," he said. His breath came with irritation that sounded like a habit more than a reaction.

Amelia took the sleeve to the forward galley and set it on a tray with a form. She filled the form in her constrained block: item, location, time.

The old paper behind the coffee machine waited like a whisper inside a wall. The scarf waited in plastic. The cabin waited, and the night kept pressing its face to the glass.

Amelia checked the curtain to first class again. It hung like a veil no one had lifted in a chapel before the vows. She kept her hands off it. She kept her posture casual. She kept her skull full of open eyes, nothing else.

The seat belt sign pinged twice and stayed lit.

A passenger near row 12, who had slept through most of the drama, raised his head and blinked at the light. "Did we land?" he asked, not to anyone in particular.

Betsy smiled at him. "Not yet," she said. "You missed the worst movie in the world. It stars anxiety and overhead bins."

He settled back with relief and drifted again.

The purser touched Amelia's elbow. "You need a minute to breathe?"

"I'll breathe when Greta is back in her seat," Amelia said.

They both knew that might not happen.

Amelia stood in the aisle and listened for the small tells, the tug of fabric, the scrape of a shoe, the breath that comes in a rhythm out of step with the plane. She counted seats, and faces, and call lights that stayed dark. She counted people who looked back with trust. She counted the threat only as far as she needed to stay sharp.

Someone brushed the curtain at the forward end. A shadow wavered, then cleared. No one emerged. The captain's voice came through a moment later, calm as ever. "Cabin crew, remain at stations for the next ten minutes."

Ten minutes can hold a lifetime on a night flight. People can dream whole lives in ten minutes and wake with salt on their cheeks. People can lose things they never meant to let go.

Amelia looked down the aisle to the scarf in its sleeve and the empty seat where tea had cooled. She turned toward the cockpit corridor once more.

A man in the bulkhead row lifted his phone and woke the screen. A photo showed a woman and a dog on a porch with peeling paint. The dog wore a bandanna. The man stroked the black rectangle as if he could pet a head through glass.

"Nice dog," Betsy said.

"She's perfect," the man said.

"Then you have to go home," Betsy said. "That's the rule with perfect dogs."

He smiled and set the phone down, face dark again.

Amelia paused at row 24C and looked at the closed shade. The seat's occupant had kept a low profile for hours. The shade itself told a story: a clean edge, no fingerprints, a smudge near the latch from older hands. No sound came through. She did not lift the shade. Everyone deserves one safe curtain until evidence asks for a different choice.

A single baby cry floated up from far aft, then went quiet as a parent rocked and hummed. The engines held their tone. The air out there didn't care about feuds or coins or gloves. It wanted lift and drag and the math that lets a city of people ride a river of wind.

Amelia stepped into the forward gap again.

The scarf's red dot stared back at her like a small eye.

"We have a problem," Deena said.

"We had one already," Amelia said.

"This looks like proof," Deena said.

Amelia nodded. "A beginning of proof."

She lifted the interphone and called the flight deck once more. Her voice did not shake. "Captain, we have a personal item with blood at your door."

The door remained a door.

The plane kept its promise to move forward through a long, dark sky.

Inside, Amelia kept hers.

Chapter 7

The cabin held a soft hush, a long hush after strain, the kind of quiet that gathers over dark water. Overhead panels glowed in a dim ribbon. Plastic cups nested on the cart like shells. The engines thrummed a steady note underfoot. Amelia stood in the forward galley, palms on cool metal, and breathed in coffee and lemon wipes and the faint trace of cinnamon from a muffin someone brought in a pocket.

She went row by row in her head, building the ledger: coin missing since the blackout, glove with A.H., two scraps of ink that matched in slant and tone, a photo that would not leave her mind. Greta still absent. The scarf near the cockpit door, a single drop, bright as a warning in a hallway light.

She tucked her pen beneath the strap on her sleeve and checked the panel again. Systems read smooth. The captain's latest note sat by the phone cradle, terse and calm. Passengers had thinned into sleep shapes, kneecaps canted toward the aisle, soft snores, headphones crooked. Night on an airplane always shrank people slightly, brought out small defenses, made secrets look heavier.

She started the snack service with Deena, no trays yet, just cups and cookies and a promise that the worst had passed.

"Can I trade my cookie for coffee?" Betsy said.

Amelia smiled.

"Keep both," Betsy said.

Amelia nodded.

A few rows back, Rita lifted a hand.

"Is the seat belt sign going to stay on?" Rita said.

"For a little while," Amelia said.

Rita looked at Nolan and rolled her eyes at herself. Nolan squeezed her hand and kissed the knuckles like a reflex.

Amelia moved the cart. She kept her pace even, built from years in narrow aisles. Her eyes tracked corners and curtains and hands that strayed near bags. She marked open bins. She marked Row 24, the C seat still a circle on her chart, half shadowed by a lowered shade.

Deena returned from the aft galley with a thumbs up. Calm for now.

Amelia set the cart brake, poured two coffees, and thought of the note in her pocket. Old score. The token. The ink looked aged, but the words felt fresh, like heat laid on a wound. She drew a tiny star in the margin of her mental page where the glove lived, A.H. stitched on its cuff, right hand, worn smooth across the palm from use, not from display.

Betsy slid into the aisle with the small bounce of someone who liked motion and strangers.

"People are sleeping again," Betsy said.

"Good," Amelia said.

"Bad for my gossip," Betsy said.

Amelia let a corner of her mouth lift. Betsy's presence, like a small night-light, kept fear from edging every seat.

She checked the water levels, refilled the coffee from the flask, and then took a breath to sit for one minute on the jumpseat. One minute only. She let her shoulders settle. Memories came like small slides: her dad crouched in a hallway when she was ten, holding a flashlight and a loose wire that buzzed, his hands steady, his voice warm, telling her that steadiness keeps others steady. She had believed him. She lived by it.

She stood again and took the manifest from the slot at the galley wall. Names in black print, aisle numbers neat as a parade. She traced highlighted marks she had added since pushback. Seat swaps. One preboard for anxiety. A blank square for 24C when the passenger ducked early behind a curtain and never reemerged while Amelia watched. She underlined Ms. Tamsin Roth, seat number intact, book in hand since boarding, a study in stillness.

She rolled the cart down the left aisle. People woke at her scent trail, cocoa and coffee, and asked shy questions about Paris, about morning there, about taxis. Small talk steadied nerves. She gave out napkins and smiled at a baby who stared at her with open wonder and a single line of drool. The baby blinked, then grinned.

She reached Ms. Roth and paused. A plain cover on the book. Worn corners, a crease across the middle as if it had ridden in a bag for years.

"Coffee?" Amelia said.

"Please," Ms. Roth said.

Amelia poured.

Ms. Roth took the cup without looking up. Her mouth formed a thank you, but her gaze stayed pinned to a page. Her hair hung blunt to one shoulder, smooth as a curtain. The right side of her face, near the eye, caught a thin line of light from the overhead, which broke on the cheekbone and shadowed her mouth. There was a ring on her index finger, old gold, flat set, a faint crest carved into it that the eye wanted to name.

Amelia moved on.

She delivered a cup to Bradley Gaines, who took it with a sigh like someone who had chewed a lemon peel.

"This flight," Bradley said.

Amelia nodded once and kept walking.

She handed a blanket to Mrs. Carmichael, whose hands trembled when she reached for it. The older woman patted the fabric, eyes bright as if secrets pressed behind them seeking release.

"Thank you," Mrs. Carmichael said.

Amelia set a cookie on Mrs. Carmichael's tray and did not ask the question that tugged. Not here. Not yet.

She pushed into the galley with the cart, locked the wheels, then took out the small notebook where she logged found items. She wrote:

- Gate scrap: left pocket, match to seat scrap. Diagonal tear. Slanted hand.

- Glove, right, A.H. embroidery. Under Lionel's seat. Left pocket with notes.

- Photo: group of young adults, coffee ring near top edge, crease line. Owner snatched back. Face on right like Lionel.

- Parchment: behind coffee machine gap, vow language, crest match to Greta's folder art.

She capped the pen. She checked her watch and added a small time stamp next to the mechanical clearance note, Captain Reeves's check cleared five minutes ago.

She returned to the aisle. She needed to feel the people again, like checking a pulse.

Rita lifted a hand.

"Do you think she's okay?" Rita said.

Amelia knew the she.

"We're looking," Amelia said.

Rita swallowed. Nolan watched Amelia as if she held a lever that could swing the plane from danger to safety by touch alone.

"Drink some water," Amelia said.

Rita nodded.

Amelia had never liked the phrase false friend. It made trust sound like a picture in a frame, hung at an angle, ready to drop at any step. Still, Lionel's words sat heavy. She scanned faces and hands and the angle of shoulders that leaned in toward aisles.

She reached the curtain near first class and paused. On the far side, a hum of conversation, then cloth drew tight and released, a breath of air in the gap, then quiet again. She let it be.

Betsy drifted up with two empty cups.

"Row twenty-three says the movie about the dog is better than the one about the doomed castle," Betsy said.

Amelia fought a smile.

"That's progress," Amelia said.

"Dog wins over doomed castle," Betsy said. "Good omen."

People laughed in small pockets, a welcome music.

Amelia turned to the manifest again and made a thin circle around Ms. Roth's seat number. Not an accusation. A reminder. When the time came to talk, she wanted that talk to start soft. Not a trap. An invitation.

She moved down the right aisle, checked the ceiling panels as she went, made sure the mask latches that sprung during the earlier bump had closed, recorded their numbers. She pressed a palm near the temperature outlet to feel the air. Warm enough.

Lionel lay two rows aft now, shifted to the last row within reach of the physician's kit. The doctor, a gray-shirted man with tired eyes, watched the monitor light that blinked on his own watch. Lionel's chest rose and fell, steady, thin. The tremor in his hand had calmed. The velvet pouch did not hang from his coat. The absence sat there like a mouth.

Amelia stood a moment too long.

The doctor looked up.

"He's holding," the doctor said.

She nodded.

She stayed until she could step away without drawing eyes.

She returned to the galley and found Deena filling three carafes.

"Keep it quiet until we have anything to tell," Deena said.

"Yes," Amelia said.

"Greta's still not in a seat," Deena said.

"We'll find her," Amelia said.

They went back out with cups and foil-topped containers. The snack service looped a second time, easier now, the rhythm back, small jokes in the galley, Deena's dry one-liners, Betsy's observations that rifled past judgment and landed in affection.

Betsy leaned against the galley wall and whispered toward Amelia's ear.

"Ms. Roth asked for black tea earlier," Betsy said. "Then sat and stared at it until it went cold."

"Tea will do that," Amelia said.

Betsy leaned away with a nod.

Amelia finished the row and cut across the galley again, slowed by the need to list. Clues lined up like coins on a table, each with a mark, a nick, a story in its metal. The urge to solve ran hot, yet she kept her hands steady, because the job came first. Safety came first. Truth lived inside safety, not the other way around.

She drifted toward Ms. Roth's row with a water bottle and a napkin, a reason to stand nearby.

Ms. Roth closed her book.

"Refill?" Amelia said.

"Thank you," Ms. Roth said.

Amelia poured. The water made a soft bloom in the paper cup and then a still puddle.

"Have you seen the lady with the folder? Brown hair, headband," Amelia said.

"Which lady?" Ms. Roth said.

"The scholar," Amelia said.

Ms. Roth sipped.

"Not since earlier," Ms. Roth said.

Amelia waited. Silence opened a space where truth sometimes stepped in.

Ms. Roth set the cup down, then lifted it again.

"Planes at night bring out old stories," Ms. Roth said.

Amelia let that hang. She gave a short nod and moved on.

At Row 24 she paused. Seat C held a jacket now, blue, folded on the cushion, no person. She memorized the brand, the shape, a small white thread near the cuff. The window shade lay low. Two rows across, a man pretended to sleep with his mouth open, but his foot tapped at an angle that told a different thing.

Deena called for more cups. Amelia returned to the galley and opened a fresh sleeve. Her hands knew the work. The cups fanned with a soft slither. The rhythm led her toward an ease she needed.

She took a moment to check the pocket where the note lived. She did not take it out. She noted its presence with a touch. She looked at the glove, also in that left pocket, and fought the impulse to match it to Lionel's right hand again in her head. The pairing existed. That was enough for now.

She looked up. Ms. Roth stood in the aisle near the galley curtain, book held against her chest like a shield.

"Do you need anything?" Amelia said.

"No," Ms. Roth said.

They stood in the quiet that galleys hold when secrets draw near but do not yet speak.

Ms. Roth's gaze shifted toward the forward corridor, toward the door where the scarf had rested earlier with that drop like a ruby. She adjusted the book against her chest.

"If she never comes back, it will be better for all of us," Ms. Roth said.

She turned and walked back to her seat.

Amelia did not follow. She held the edge of the cart and let the engine note fill her bones again. Better for all of us carried a shape that did not match the tone she wanted for this night. She filed the words under the line she had drawn around Ms. Roth's name. She underlined the circle once.

She looked down the cabin. Faces shifted in dreams. Couples leaned into each other like ropes that held in a storm. A boy hugged a plastic dinosaur. A man blinked at a screen, then at the window, then at nothing in between. The plane carried them all toward a dawn that would come in a different city. Somewhere forward, hidden by bulkhead and doors and rules that guarded judgment, the cockpit held two steady figures who kept everyone aloft.

Amelia squared the cart and pushed back into service. She moved with the confidence of someone who had chosen a path and kept it in sight even when the floor shivered. She was not a detective. She was a flight attendant who took care of people. On this night, that meant questions and notes and a calm face that asked others to match it. It meant keeping a ledger, tight and factual, until one line turned bold and answered every other line.

She checked the clock again and wrote the time near her last entry. Then she turned a cup upright, poured, and gave it to a woman who said thank you like a prayer. She smiled back. A small thing, but it changed the air.

Chapter 8

The scream rose from the forward corridor, sharp as a cut in canvas, and every head in the first rows lifted at once. Cups rattled. A spoon slid off a tray with a dry ring. Amelia moved before her mind caught the details, body reading the sound as a summons.

She reached the curtain and pulled it back. The corridor felt narrow, the walls close. Greta sat slumped on the carpet near the cockpit door, her back to the bulkhead, one hand at her collar. A small bloom of blood marked the edge of her shirt, not much, but bright. Papers lay in a messy arc around her knees.

"Help," Greta said.

Amelia dropped to a knee beside her. Deena rushed up with a gauze pad from the kit. The physician arrived three strides behind, breath even, case in hand, eyes already locked to the wound.

"Hold this," the doctor said.

Amelia pressed the pad at Greta's collarbone while Deena steadied Greta's shoulder. The skin felt hot. Greta's eyes tried to fix on Amelia's face, then skated, then fixed again.

"You're safe," Amelia said.

Greta swallowed and worked for breath through the pinch of pain.

"Someone pushed me," Greta said.

The physician cleaned the area and found a shallow cut above the clavicle. Scalp unbroken, pupils equal, breath even enough. He glanced at Amelia.

"She's stable," the doctor said.

The corridor drew people by gravity. Heads rose over shoulders at the curtain edge. A baby cried once in a seat and then went quiet, as if the sound had startled itself.

Amelia looked down at the scatter of pages. A glimmer winked at the edge of a page near Greta's heel. The small round metal shape sat half hidden by a folded chart. She reached and lifted it. The coin lay in her palm, heavier than she expected. Worn rim. Crest engraved with care. A tiny nick at about ten o'clock, exactly as she had logged. Across its face ran three faint scratches she did not remember, thin as cat marks.

She closed her fingers around it and looked at Greta.

"Where did it come from?" Amelia said.

Greta blinked at the coin.

"They took it," Greta said. "Then dropped papers... I bent to save the pages... it fell there."

"Who took it?" Amelia said.

Greta's jaw tightened. She worked her tongue across a split in her lip.

"I know the face," Greta said.

"Say the name," Amelia said.

"Not yet," Greta said. "Not until I can prove it."

"We need the truth now," Amelia said.

Greta winced.

"They want us to fight each other," Greta said. "That's the proof they need."

Amelia slid the coin into her right pocket and pressed her hand against it. The metal held a mild warmth from her skin. She looked at Deena.

"Keep them back," Amelia said.

Deena stepped into the aisle with open hands, palms low, voice even, turned toward the crowd.

"Give us room," Deena said.

Amelia collected the pages near Greta's knee and stacked them, not neat, but enough to control. The top sheet bore a tree of names and thin lines, some crossed with dark strokes. Rightful owner. Final reconciliation. Words like stones.

Ms. Roth stepped forward, book still in her hand, eyes wide.

"Is she okay?" Ms. Roth said.

"She will be," Amelia said.

Tamsin hesitated, then reached for a page that had slid under Greta's shoe.

"I know how to handle old paper," Ms. Roth said.

Amelia looked at her for a beat and then nodded.

"Careful," Amelia said.

They gathered the documents. Greta watched with quick, hot eyes.

"Don't trust the obvious ally," Greta said.

"Who is that?" Amelia said.

"The one who smiles when you look, then watches when you turn away," Greta said.

Amelia filed the phrase. She did not look at Ms. Roth. She kept her hands moving. She let the coin sit against her palm like a promise she would not share yet.

Captain Reeves called from the cockpit door, voice calm, posture square in the narrow frame.

"Status?" the captain said.

"Minor cut," the doctor said. "She's lucid."

The captain nodded and turned a fraction toward the panel behind him, then back.

"We stay on plan," the captain said.

Betsy hovered behind the second curtain with a blanket.

"Do you want this for the floor?" Betsy said.

"Yes," Amelia said.

Betsy laid the blanket beneath Greta's legs. Her face went soft at the sight of the blood spot, then firm again.

"Who did it?" Betsy said.

Greta shut her eyes and opened them. The cut had slowed.

"I saw their face," Greta said.

"Say the name," Betsy said.

Greta shook her head.

"Give me one minute," Greta said. "I need to place the proof where they cannot twist it."

Amelia watched the doctor tape the gauze. The press of fingers brought a hiss from Greta, then calm again.

"We'll move you aft," the doctor said.

"Not yet," Greta said.

"Yes," Amelia said.

Greta looked up at Amelia.

"You hold the coin?" Greta said.

"I do," Amelia said.

"Keep it hidden," Greta said. "If it pairs with the wrong hands, this never ends."

"How do we end it?" Amelia said.

Greta's gaze went to the stack of papers and then to Amelia's pocket.

"By keeping them apart until we land," Greta said. "By believing the person who has nothing to gain."

Amelia rose and scanned the faces at the curtain line. Bradley stood near the aisle, jaw set, eyes on the coin pocket as if he could see through cloth. A young man craned for a better angle. Mrs. Carmichael held the edge of the curtain, lips pressed.

"Back to your seats," Amelia said.

Bradley did not move.

"Now," Amelia said.

Bradley took a step backward, then turned and went three rows, eyes still on Amelia.

Ms. Roth handed over the paper she had rescued.

"Thank you," Amelia said.

Ms. Roth nodded. She did not smile.

Amelia and Deena lifted Greta with care. The physician took her other side. They walked her back along the aisle as the plane breathed around them. People watched with the intensity of a theater audience at a third act, when the play starts to look like the world they know.

They settled Greta in the same last-row cluster where the doctor could monitor both patients. Greta's breath eased. The doctor adjusted the sling on the blood pressure cuff and checked the reading. He looked at Amelia and gave a small nod.

Amelia leaned close to Greta's ear.

"Was it a man?" Amelia said.

"Yes," Greta said.

"Older or younger?" Amelia said.

"Not young," Greta said.

"Passenger or crew?" Amelia said.

"Passenger," Greta said.

"Did he say anything?" Amelia said.

Greta blinked slow.

"He used the word claim as if it had a lock on it," Greta said.

Amelia straightened.

"Keep the papers with you," Amelia said.

Greta touched the stack with a small protectiveness that made Amelia ache. Not for the papers. For the life that used them as armor.

Amelia turned to go, then paused.

"If you think of the name," Amelia said.

"I will call you," Greta said.

Amelia moved through the curtain and into the nearer rows. She could feel the coin in her pocket like a pulse. People's eyes jumped from her to each other, then away, then back again. The hum of engines filled gaps that words could break.

Rita pulled Amelia close with a look.

"Is she going to be okay?" Rita said.

"She will," Amelia said.

"Was it a passenger?" Nolan said.

"Go ahead and sit tight," Amelia said.

She kept moving. The plane needed her movement more than it needed answers in that moment.

She reached the forward galley to start a quick clean of blood from the floor. Betsy stood with a bottle and a rag.

"I can do that," Betsy said.

"I have it," Amelia said.

They worked together in silence until the corridor looked like an ordinary walkway again.

The phone on the galley wall buzzed. Amelia lifted the receiver.

"Flight deck," Captain Reeves said. "You have a moment?"

"Yes," Amelia said.

"We've got a call from the aft," the captain said. "Doctor wants you. Lionel's numbers want attention."

On cue, the cabin speakers pinged with a polite chime. A murmur rippled like wind over grain. People who had drawn closer to watch now slid back into rows as if moved by a slow tide.

Amelia glanced toward the last rows. The doctor looked her way and lifted two fingers, a sign of urgency that did not set panic loose but did place weight on her next steps.

She spoke into the phone.

"I'm coming," Amelia said.

She slipped the receiver back into its cradle and pressed two fingers to the coin in her pocket. Fresh scratches on the face. The tool that made them would leave kin marks elsewhere. On a panel. On a hatch. On a wire. The story would tie to edges. It always did.

She started aft. Ms. Roth watched her pass. Bradley also watched, his mouth tight.

Mrs. Carmichael lowered her eyes as Amelia approached, but not before a flick of recognition crossed her face at the bulge in Amelia's pocket. Not greed. Not fear. Something older than either, a tug from years.

Amelia kept walking. The aisle felt long, the line of seats an alley with a thousand doors. She let the hum hold her steady. She carried the coin like a trust for strangers she cared about as if they were her family. The night had length yet in it. She would stand through it.

At the aft curtain she drew a breath, then slipped through to the last row where the doctor held Lionel's wrist and checked count against the watch that pulsed on his own vein. Greta watched with a hard gaze that looked ready to rise again if the world asked for it.

"His pulse dropped, then returned," the doctor said.

"Does he need oxygen?" Amelia said.

"I am giving it now," the doctor said.

Amelia set a hand on the seatback and leaned to Lionel's level. His eyes opened as if pulled by a string.

"Mr. Hughes," Amelia said.

"Don't let them," Lionel said. "Don't let them... the past..."

His eyes slid shut. The doctor adjusted the mask and the line.

A chime pinged from the flight deck again. The captain's voice, smooth and even, walked down the cabin.

"Folks, please stay seated while we assist a passenger," the captain said. "We appreciate your patience."

Amelia watched Lionel settle. She felt the coin against her leg. She looked at Greta, who nodded once, fiercely.

They had breathed through the scream. They had brought the coin back into sight with new wounds on its face. The attacker still lived behind a curtain or a posture or a friendly line that did not belong. The night would give more.

The galley phone buzzed again. Deena reached it first, then looked at Amelia.

"Flight deck," Deena said. "Captain wants a quick word. Urgent."

Amelia squeezed the coin. The plane flew on. The edge had shifted again. Two fronts at once.

She went forward to meet the call.

Chapter 9

The cabin glowed in a blue haze, screens muted, eyes heavy, the engine's steady hum a tide against the ribs. A plastic cup trembled on Lionel's tray with a thin ring of water, widening, tightening, as the monitor beside him hiccupped a stutter of light.

"Sir?" Amelia said.

The physician, a compact man with kind eyes and a travel cardigan, already had two fingers along Lionel's neck. "Pulse," he said. "Weak, present."

Lionel's skin had the color of old paper. A faint bruise shadowed the inside of his right forearm, small and round. Amelia took in the mark, then the slackness of his mouth, the beads of sweat at his temple. The smear of fear around him felt like ozone before a storm, the air changed in a way you taste at the back of the tongue.

"Let's move him aft," the physician said. "Less foot traffic."

She nodded. Deena appeared with a blanket and a blood-pressure cuff. Together they eased Lionel from the row, passengers lifting knees, twisting shoulders. The aisle felt narrow as a gullet. A woman crossed herself. A teen pulled out earbuds and stared, wide and solemn.

"Careful with his arm," Amelia said.

They settled him in the last row by the galley, a seat that could shelter him from the attention that chews hope. The cuff hissed. The physician checked the tiny portable monitor again, then glanced at her. "Oxygen."

Amelia fit the mask over Lionel's face. His eyelids fluttered. He spoke something inside the mask that came like a sigh that missed its mark.

"What was that?" she asked.

He swallowed. "Don't let them," he said, thin as thread. "The past."

She smoothed the blanket, then looked to the physician. He answered with a quiet nod: stable for this minute, which was all any minute ever promised.

She called the flight deck, keeping her voice even. "We have a medical event, passenger mid-forties. Pulse weak but steady. Oxygen on."

Captain Reeves answered through a faint crackle. "Copy. Patch me updates. We're over the water midpoint. Closest options are limited. If he crashes, we divert. Otherwise we hold for Paris."

A hush crawled out from the aft row, creeping forward. Some people sleep with one ear open. Even a whisper of emergency changes posture, changes breath. Betsy Kwon stood, then sat again, then stood, then thought better of it and stayed in place, hands tucked under thighs like a kid on a cold bench.

Amelia watched the bruise on Lionel's forearm, tidy, coin-small, out of place on a man who'd done no physical work tonight except worry.

Deena leaned in low. "You see that?"

She answered with a soft sound that meant yes and wait.

The seat-belt chime gave one sad ping, then fell silent. The plane smoothed out. Everyone listened to silence as if it might say more.

Captain Reeves made a brief announcement that danced on the edge of bland on purpose: a passenger felt unwell, a physician was assisting, the crew had it in hand. Calm words are a cloth you throw over a fire to cut the oxygen.

Near row twenty-two, Bradley Gaines turned in his seat and lifted his hands in a small theater of impatience. "Unbelievable."

It wasn't loud. It still carried. Amelia's smile formed by habit and training, the one that kept edges from cutting.

"Sir," she said. "Seat belt, please."

He clicked it without looking at her, eyes on the aisle where Lionel had been.

Rita and Nolan, the honeymooners, clutched each other shoulder to hip, like a single person made awkward by seams. "Is he dying?" Rita asked.

"He's in good hands," Amelia said. "We're watching him."

"Will we land somewhere else?" Nolan asked.

"We'll go where the captain decides is safest."

Betsy raised a hand in a small wave. "I have mints if anyone needs a mint," she said. "I always feel better with a mint." It bought a smile from two rows and changed the air a shade.

From a few rows up, Mrs. Carmichael's face turned toward the aft like a sunflower turning when light shifts. Her eyes found Amelia, then dropped, then found her again. The older woman's hands folded over the strap of her purse. A tremor passed through the knuckles, then stilled.

Amelia took the small windowed envelope from Lionel's carry-on. She'd seen it when moving him: PARIS, 1982, written in ink that had browned a little, the way people brown a little. She didn't open things without reason. Tonight felt like reason.

She showed it to the physician first. He nodded and returned his eyes to Lionel.

The envelope gave a sigh at the glue line. Two letters slid into her hand, paper soft enough to remember the fingers that held it thirty years ago. The handwriting leaned forward like a man in a hurry. Broken promise. Blood debt. She held the edges, not the words. Some phrases echo when they shouldn't: debts and tokens and old scores. Her pocket held the scrap from the gate, the other from under a seat. Same slanted hand. Same stubborn tilt.

A shadow interrupted the aisle. Dr. Greta Morrison, hair tucked back with a rubber band that had given up halfway through its life, stood just out of the light's center. "May I... help?" she asked. "I know the history. I could—"

"History later," Amelia said.

Greta nodded once, guilt and worry both on her face. Her hands trembled at rest the way some hands tremble in action.

Mrs. Carmichael stood now, steadying herself with the seat-top as if the air changed weight. She took small steps aft. Amelia met her halfway in the narrow, where two people become one shape.

"Child," the older woman said, "you opened the 1982 envelope. I knew a boy then. He took something that wasn't his because he believed no one would ever call the debt. He had no sense for time: that it rolls back."

"Was his name Lionel?" Amelia asked.

"Not then." Mrs. Carmichael looked toward the galley where the oxygen hissed. "He wore another name. The coin wasn't money. It was a key. That family never stopped fighting. De Riviere, I think. They were in Paris the summer the river flooded. Fights over old houses. Papers with seals. Always the same words: return, rightful, blood." She pressed her lips together, then found a brittle smile. "I taught in a village where grudges age slower than wine."

"Is Lionel from that family?"

"I couldn't swear," she said. "But I recognize the look on a man who carries a door key he can't bear to use." Her gaze dropped to the letters in Amelia's hand. "You'll find threats wrapped in grace in there. The way snakes move in grass and you see only grass."

"Thank you," Amelia said.

The older woman touched her elbow, then returned to her seat with careful steps.

Amelia read enough to confirm the pattern. A promise broken in 1982. A meeting set near a bridge. The phrase blood debt, written without drama, almost with relief, like a confession of a thing already decided. The exact language from the scraps. A chain of hands and pens across years.

"Any change?" she asked the physician.

"Pressure holding," he said. "Pulse gaining a little."

"Okay."

Captain Reeves called back again. "Status?"

"Stable," she said. "We're still Paris-bound."

"Good."

A drink cart rattled behind curtains. Deena peeked in. "You want water, coffee?"

"Water," Amelia said. "For the physician. And me."

Bradley stood when she turned. "This is ridiculous," he said. "We should divert. Or we should not. Choose. This limbo is a joke."

Amelia kept the smile. "Please sit, sir. We'll update everyone when we have more."

Bradley sank into his seat. "He brought this on himself," he muttered. "The dramatics. These things don't just happen."

Betsy whispered, "He's angry because he's scared," then held out a mint. "Still helps."

Amelia studied the cabin the way a mechanic studies a vibration. Subtle signs matter more than the obvious. Ms. Tamsin Roth watched from her seat with a book in her lap, unread, a ribbon tucked between pages. She had the stillness of someone who could sit two hours without twitching. Rita and Nolan leaned forehead to forehead. Mrs. Carmichael's gaze shifted between Amelia and Lionel with an ache behind it. Greta hovered, a scholar without a podium.

"Can we talk?" Greta asked, low, when Amelia came near.

"Briefly."

"The coin marks a claim," Greta said. "I said that before. It's more exact than claim. Some families used tokens when land broke into pieces. A token answered a riddle built into a will. Whoever held it could unlock language that otherwise meant nothing. It's theater with teeth."

"Who else knows the riddle?"

"Anyone who can read old French and trace branches of a tree," Greta said. "So, a few of us. And a few who pretend."

"Where did you learn it?"

"At a museum and in letters a colleague shared." Greta's mouth pressed thin. "If someone injected him, it means someone decided the play needed a silence."

Amelia thought of the bruise. "If."

Greta dipped her head. "If," she said. "I want him alive. For him. And also because dead men fit too easily into the stories other people want to tell."

A chime. Captain Reeves again. "Cabin ready?"

"Ready," she said, scanning seat belts, latches, faces. Ready felt like a word you say to keep your hands from shaking.

She returned to the honeymooners. "How are you two?"

"Scared," Rita said. "He's worse, isn't he?"

"He's steady," Amelia said. "He needs quiet."

Nolan touched the back of Rita's hand, then leaned toward Amelia with a cautious look. "Can I say something? Before boarding, she..." he tipped his head toward Ms. Roth, "talked on her phone in three different languages. Fast. All business. She mentioned Paris and papers. Maybe nothing." His face flushed. "I hate to live as that guy who reports people. It just popped in my head now because—"

"You did fine to share," Amelia said. "Thank you."

She logged the tip in her mind beside the 1982 letters, the bruise, the coin, the old woman's story. Every piece carried a weight. Sometimes pieces clicked. Sometimes they cluttered.

Betsy leaned out into the aisle as Amelia passed. "Cross-check last names," she murmured. "Old family names hide in plain sight. I have a gift for names. Not numbers." She grinned. "I keep receipts forever because math scares me."

"Thank you," Amelia said, and kept moving.

She took one more look at Lionel. His chest lifted under the blanket in small climbs, small descents. The physician offered a nod and what could pass for a smile on a man counting seconds.

Amelia tucked the letters back into their envelope and slid it under the strap of Lionel's carry-on. The coin was not here. The coin had moved through hands and air, then vanished in a darkness with timing too neat to call chance.

She checked with Captain Reeves again. He sounded steady. "Hold course," he said. "We're two hours out."

"Copy."

Her radio hissed with a burst of breath that wasn't hers. She lifted it closer. The noise cut, returned, then became a voice that wore a scarf. "Meet me in the aft galley," it said. "Come alone."

She looked down the aisle where a few reading lights burned like small moons. She looked at Deena, who was pouring water into a cup with care as if not to wake it. She looked at Lionel and the physician and then at the curtain.

"Who is this?" she asked.

Silence pressed in, thick and deliberate. The channel clicked dead.

She set the radio down and felt the cabin gather itself. You learn a plane's body the way you learn a friend's mood. Every sound had a meaning. Every pause had one, too.

Chapter 10

The aft galley held the hush of a chapel at night. Metal racks gleamed in low light. Coffee smelled like a promise left open too long. Amelia slipped behind the curtain. A figure waited in the wedge between carts, hood up, scarf high. Nothing to see but eyes, quick and intelligent.

"You asked for me," Amelia said.

"I asked for the only one not playing." The voice could have been male or female. It wore a rasp that might be labor or habit.

"Then talk."

"You don't want a big truth right now," the figure said. "Big truths make people bleed. Here's a small one: the coin is a proof. So is something like a cameo. Whoever holds both writes the ending."

"Who wants the ending their way?"

"More than one. Old families rot from the root outward. No one sees it until the branches fall." The eyes shifted past her toward the curtain, then back. "If you force a name now, you'll trigger a move. Wait, and you might pick who lands alive."

"Did you touch Lionel?" Amelia asked.

"No." The scarf dipped. "I warned him to hand the token to a neutral hand. He laughed at the word neutral. Imagine that."

"You recognized the attacker who hurt Greta?"

"I can't prove it yet," the figure said. "You'll hear a dozen claims about rightful blood. Half are paper. Half are theater. Listen for the ones who use words like vow and debt as if they mean prayer." A breath. "I'll come back."

"Tell me your name."

"You already know me," the figure said. "Everyone knows me. They just never listened."

A shout cut the dark. "Thief!" Bradley's voice, sharp as a snapped blade.

Amelia pushed through the curtain. The aisle yanked her forward like a current. Bradley stood at row twenty-four with his overhead bin open, face hot, hair out of place for the first time all night. He pointed at Ms. Roth. "She went through my case," he said. "She took a folder."

Tamsin Roth looked up slow, then stood. She held her book at her side. Calm covered her like cloth. "I touched nothing of yours," she said.

"You're a liar."

"Sir," Amelia said, stepping between them. "Sit, please. Ms. Roth, you too."

"She's a plant," Bradley said. "She's been working angles since we left the gate. I saw her near my bag."

"You saw me near my seat," Tamsin said. "Your bag roosted two rows back because you arrived late and shoved people aside. Sit down."

Bradley flung a hand toward the open bin. "She removed a folder."

Deena reached the row at a jog and peered into the bin. The case sat open inside, papers in a state that could be called rummaged or simply used. "Sir, what exactly is missing?" she asked.

"A folder with contracts."

"Contracts," Tamsin said, dry. "From which decade?"

He glared at her, then at Amelia. "I want her searched."

"No," Amelia said. "We don't search passengers. We can look for your folder." She scanned the seat pockets, the floor, the crevice between cushion and shell. Nothing. She bent, lifted the case. The hinge bore a smear of brass from friction and a nick that looked fresh. She closed it, reopened it. "Was it locked?"

Bradley made a face. "The lock sticks."

"Then it wasn't locked," Betsy said from the aisle, cheeks pink with worry and nose. "You can't blame a lock if it's not a lock."

"Sit," Amelia said, voice firm now. "Both of you."

Captain Reeves' voice filled the cabin. "Ladies and gentlemen, please stay seated. We have a minor cabin disturbance we'll resolve shortly." Minor is another cloth. He knew it. She knew it.

Amelia addressed Bradley low. "If you're missing a folder, give me the color and label. We'll look calmly."

He stared another second at Tamsin like a man trying to set her on fire by will, then ground out, "Blue. Tab labeled KESTREL."

Deena scribbled it on a service napkin as if writing on linen could anchor a thing. "Blue. KESTREL. Got it."

Amelia turned to Tamsin. "Did you see anyone near here in the last fifteen minutes? Anyone who didn't belong on this row?"

"I saw plenty of people who don't belong anywhere," Tamsin said. She let the hint of a smile show and then let it fade. "A man stood right over my head not five minutes ago. Tall, square shoulders, suit that tried too hard. I couldn't see his face because he kept the brim of his cap low like a boy hiding on a school bus."

"Did he open the bin?"

"Yes," she said. "But I assumed you knew him. He moved the way crew move when they're late for trays."

Bradley made a sound in his throat like a hinge rubbing dry. "You expect anyone to believe that?"

Betsy lifted her hand in that small wave again. "I saw someone too," she said. "Not her. More like a silhouette. Maybe a sports coat. Definitely not a cardigan." She tilted her head at the physician in rueful apology. "No offense."

"None taken," the physician said from the back, eyes still on Lionel.

"Okay," Amelia said. "We'll sweep nearby rows for a blue folder."

They checked the bin above twenty-five. Nothing. Checked twenty-three. Nothing. Looked along the carpet for the edge of a tab that had slid. Nothing. The aisle grew crowded with eyes. People can stay seated and still lean into a story.

Captain Reeves stepped into the aisle long enough to give it gravity. "Sir, ma'am," he said to Bradley and Tamsin. "If you force the issue, I will have you restrained. We're not far from our destination. Let's not make poor choices we will all regret when someone asks us to explain them."

Bradley sat hard. Tamsin folded into her seat with the grace of a cat who hates the box but will stand inside it a moment to show she's a good sport.

Amelia crouched by Bradley's case and closed it. She held his gaze. "Keep this at your feet," she said.

"I pay for overhead space," he said.

"You pay for the seat, too," Betsy said under her breath. "Use the whole package."

A ripple of tired amusement traveled three seats in both directions and took a little of the heat with it.

Amelia returned to the galley. The hooded informant had dissolved back into passenger. Shadows don't hold their shape long when you need them most. She pushed the curtain aside and went in with two long breaths.

On the floor near the service phone lay a folded piece of paper, clean edges, cheap stock. It must have fallen when she came through, or someone slipped it while the aisle had turned to theater. She picked it up with a napkin, unfolding it with care.

Block letters stared up from the page. THE NEXT LIFE CLAIMED IS ON YOUR HANDS IF YOU KEEP DIGGING.

She set the paper on a tray. The letters were too neat to be panic, too stiff to be art. A hand had worked to hide itself. The ink sank dark into the fibers. It had none of the age of 1982, none of the lean forward script. A modern threat that hated curves.

Deena stepped in, voice low. "Anything?"

Amelia showed her the page.

Deena breathed through her nose, then said, "They always write like that in movies. Why do they write like that now?"

"Because they think it hides them," Amelia said. "Because they like the look."

"It's taped together from TV," Deena said. "Not life."

"Tonight they want TV," Amelia said. "So the cabin looks one way and the truth looks another."

The service phone buzzed. Amelia grabbed it, keeping the paper ironed flat with her other hand. "Galley."

The captain again. "We're steady. Keep the lid on."

"We'll try."

Amelia ended the call and flicked the curtain. Bradley peered back at her with a knife of a stare. Tamsin studied nothing at all like a woman counting breath. Mrs. Carmichael sat very still, mouth tight, as if she'd finally found the center of a shape she'd only traced before. Greta closed her eyes for one long beat and opened them glassy with hurt and fire.

Amelia took the threat note and slid it into a clean evidence bag they used when passengers dropped pills or rings. She labeled the bag with time and row and her initials. The motion soothed her the way washing a mug does after a funeral. Small order inside large defeat.

She returned to Lionel, made a small adjustment to the blanket, and checked the line on the portable monitor. The physician's mouth eased. "He's holding," he said. "You're doing fine."

"No," Amelia said, and let a thin smile rise. "You're doing fine. I'm just keeping the stage clear."

He chuckled once, a soft bark that said fatigue and gratitude wore the same jacket.

She walked the aisle again, not to spy, not to threaten, just to be a body that kept the space safe. People watched her the way people watch a lighthouse through fog: if the light keeps moving, you can forgive the fog.

Ms. Roth looked up when Amelia reached her row. "You found a note," Tamsin said. "You haven't told me, but I can tell. Your walk changed."

"You spoke three languages before boarding," Amelia said, keeping her voice soft. "Phones remember who heard us. Who were you calling?"

"Paris," Tamsin said. "And London. And a sister in Boston who thinks I should marry someone dull. She might be right."

"Business calls?"

"Some. Some not. My family keeps odd hours when inheritance goes stale."

"So you're not surprised by this flight."

Tamsin's eyes did not waver. "I'm never surprised by a family that eats itself."

"Did you remove Bradley's folder?"

"No."

"Did you see who did?"

"Not a face." She lifted the ribbon from her book and twisted it once. "Listen. You keep assuming the loudest man is the most dangerous. Sometimes the most dangerous is the man who learned to sound like a pastor."

"Who is that?"

"You'll know him when you hear him call sin by another name."

Amelia filed the words without letting them land hard. She didn't let any single thing land hard tonight. You place them on a table in your mind and see which ones fit close.

At the back, Lionel stirred. His hand lifted and tugged at the mask, then fell. He formed a word that didn't make it out. The physician bent and leaned close to catch it. A second later he looked at Amelia with a thin slice of hope. "He's coming up," he said. "Very slow. But up."

She nodded and took a final sweep through the cabin, ending at the galley where the block letters waited inside plastic. She set the bag into a drawer and closed it with a small click.

Her radio crackled again, that same scarfed voice returning without breath this time. "You came," it said. "Good. One last thing."

"I'm here."

"More than one heir on this plane," the voice said. "More than one person willing to cut the cord that ties them to the past, except the cord is a throat."

"Give me a name."

"Not yet."

"Give me a reason to trust you."

"I'm the only one who didn't ask you to choose a side."

The channel went dead. Amelia stood with the drawer under her hand and the hiss of air through vents soft as a winter river under ice. She looked out through the slit where the curtain didn't meet and watched the aisle go still, then stir again, then settle.

She brought the physician a cup of water with a lid. He took it, nodded, and smiled with the corners of his eyes. She touched the back of the last row as if it were a shoulder and stepped forward to Betsy, who held up another mint like a flag of truce.

"Take it," Betsy said. "For luck."

Amelia took it and felt its shape in her palm: a small round thing with an imprint like a coin, nothing precious and still a comfort.

She slid the mint into her pocket beside the 1982 letters, then lifted the service phone once more.

"Flight deck," she said. "Galley."

"Go ahead," Captain Reeves said.

"We're steady," she said. "But we're not."

He made a sound that might have been a laugh on a better day. "Copy," he said. "Hold."

The aisle murmured. A baby fussed and then quieted. Ms. Roth turned the page she had not read. Bradley smoothed his tie for no one. Mrs. Carmichael blinked at something only she could see, a bridge over a river, a boy with a false name, a coin's edge nicked at ten o'clock, a story that refused to die.

Amelia looked toward the curtain again. The note in the drawer waited with its square letters. The coin still lay somewhere between hands and hunger. The plane flew on toward a city where old stone never forgets and morning light can feel like proof.

The radio at her hip rested against bone. The words on the paper echoed nothing old. Modern threat. New ink. A fresh match in a room filled with dry wood.

She breathed in, breathed out, and chose to keep moving.

Chapter 11

T he galley held the scent of hot plastic and lemon wipe, a clean mask over nerves. The cabin hummed on a single note, a careful song that kept fear from finding its own voice. Amelia rested her hand on the counter edge where the surface turned cool from the air stream and listened to the soft clink of cups settling in their racks.

Deena stood shoulder to shoulder with her, the threat note flat between them like a wound that refused to close.

"It was planted in his case," Deena said. "He swears."

"He swears a lot," Amelia said.

Bradley lurked three rows back, arms folded, eyes on them like the lighting could carry heat. He had a talent for outrage, a way to claim the aisle as a stage without raising his volume. The note said a next life would be on someone's hands if they kept digging. Not if. When.

Betsy slid in, bright as always, carrying a stack of cups and a paper-thin smile. "If we run out of decaf, full revolt."

"We are not running out of decaf," Amelia said.

"We are not," Betsy said. "But also, row twenty-six is whispering about heirs, like a soap with subtitles."

Amelia kept her voice even. "What did you hear."

"'Make sure the rightful heir never lands in Paris.' That line, clean as a bell. Then a cough."

"Which seat," Deena asked.

"Hard to pin with the hush and the blanket cave. Middle of the row. Two figures tucked under."

Amelia looked past the curtain. The lights stayed low. Faces took shape as small moons, pallid and private. The aisle tempted anyone willing to risk a step. She thought of the coin's fresh scratches, the planted tool someone had used to make them, the long chain of hands that wanted a right to something that did not belong to the sky.

She crossed to the PA panel and reached under the lip. The plastic trim shifted with a tiny rasp. Not much, but off. Codes and panels had a feel, a right way of sitting. A loose bite meant a hand had been where it did not belong.

"Captain, panel feels loose," she said into the handset, quiet, clipped.

"Copy," Captain Reeves replied. "We will keep the sign on for a few while you check. No drama."

"No drama," she said, and eased the trim.

A slip of wire lay like a hair, one end frayed to a copper brush. Someone had worried it. The cable nearby showed a shallow nick. Tucked farther in, she found a pocket tool no longer than her thumb, narrow and sharp at one end, with a ridge that would fit a panel screw. The metal bore a tiny burr, a cusp that matched the scratch pattern on the coin in her memory. She lifted the tool with a napkin and set it on a tray.

Deena leaned closer. "That thing could scrape silver. Or sever patience."

Betsy peered over and whispered, "That looks like the thing my cousin uses to fix eyeglasses."

"Then our saboteur shops in the same aisle," Amelia said.

She slid the panel trim back into place and felt for the click. It did not seat clean, not yet, but the threat was out.

Tamsin Roth stood at the curtain's edge, book closed, finger inside the pages to save her place. She wore a sweater the color of the ocean when the moon kept its light to itself. Her gaze went to the tool. Then to Amelia's face.

"I did not touch any panel," Tamsin said.

Betsy answered before Amelia. "You passed this spot earlier."

"I walked by," Tamsin said. "I can walk by without changing the airplane."

"People see what they expect," Amelia said, letting the line lie there, because she had to keep her voice even in the galley at night. "May I ask where you were ten minutes ago."

"In my seat," Tamsin said. "Reading. Trying to keep my mind from going places it should not."

Bradley's voice carried from his row with that careful tilt that made it fast to hear. "Ask her about the folder. Ask her where it went."

Deena moved toward him. "Sit back, sir. We are working."

Rita and Nolan watched from their island of two seats, hands laced, eyes wide. Nolan tried a smile that had more hope than teeth. "We brought the kind of honeymoon where nothing happens," he said softly to Amelia when she passed. "We will tip the universe on the way back."

"Put it in writing," she said. Nolan actually laughed, small and real, and Rita pressed her cheek to his shoulder.

Mrs. Carmichael lifted her hand like a student from an older school. "Ms. Hart," she said, her voice a wavering ribbon. "A word, dear."

Amelia knelt so the woman would not have to pitch her voice. The older eyes were wet, not from tears, more from memory that had not asked to be stirred.

"I taught French history to a boy named Bradley," Mrs. Carmichael said. "Years ago. He asked for extra readings on certain families. He took notes as if a clock ticked behind him. Ms. Roth wrote me once, too, about records from a parish archive. She did not ask for money. She asked for a name no one wanted to say."

"Why not say it now," Amelia asked.

The woman drew breath. "Alastair," she said. "I say it at last. It never brought good things."

A chime pinged at the far end, a call light bright on the ceiling like a sudden idea. Betsy went, gliding more than walking.

Amelia returned to the galley and found Deena with a folded scrap in her palm, a new one.

"Found this in the first-class galley by the coffee lids," Deena said. "Block letters again." She opened it. The ink looked rushed. The line had a tremor: In blood, a debt is settled.

"That is two," Amelia said. "Different from the 1982 hand."

"Different," Deena said. "Same promise."

A paper breeze brushed her arm. Greta stood in the aisle, pale but upright, a bandage low in her hairline. She carried a folder like a fragile organ. Her hands shook, not from fear alone, more from the strain of holding an arc of years in single pages.

"Ms. Hart," Greta said. "Please. I found a page tucked where it should not have been. It is from a private diary, early last century. It shows the de Riviere branches and where one line broke off."

She offered the page. Amelia read the careful hand, the tree of names, the forked line, the margin note: another branch in England after a winter marriage, thin blood but still blood. A name farther down that matched Tamsin's grandmother's maiden name.

Greta watched Amelia's eyes track the lines. "I am not the villain here," Greta said. "I am guilty of obsession. Not theft."

"Who tucked the page," Amelia asked.

Greta shook her head. "The page was not in my folder when we boarded. It was slid under the flap after the scream, when I was still on the floor. Someone wanted this to surface. Or to burn someone else."

Betsy returned with a blanket over one arm and an ironic tilt of her head. "Row twenty-six's cough has an opinion," she said. "They think whoever lands in Paris with the token will claim everything. Half the row wants to be that person."

"They cannot all be right," Amelia said.

"Of course not," Betsy said. "But they can all be loud."

Amelia breathed through a slow count. She took the tool on the tray, bagged it with a zip from the cart, and logged the time on the L&F sheet, because order helped when truth did not. The hum of the airplane held. The ceiling lights put out their careful hush.

She found Tamsin again, still at the curtain, still with the book braced in her hand, the kind of reader who kept her place by feel.

"Walk with me," Amelia said.

Tamsin looked at the blanket of faces. Then at Amelia. "All right."

They moved into the narrow space near the service door where the cold gathered. The door skin held a thin frost at its lower edge. Tires would hit Paris glass in hours if they kept the machine honest. Amelia set the diary page on the counter where Tamsin could see it without grabbing.

"This branch," Amelia said. "It shows a line that could be yours."

Tamsin read faster than she breathed. Her mouth pressed flat. "It could be," she said. "It is not proof."

"You were near the panel," Amelia said. "Betsy saw you pass. Someone planted a tool. Wires were nicked."

"Then find the person with the kit," Tamsin said. "Find the hand that writes in block letters when the cabin shakes."

"You spoke earlier," Amelia said. "About the missing scholar. You said if she did not come back, it would be better for all. Why say it."

"I said it to a man who pressured me at the gate to give up claims he believes are his," Tamsin said. "I was angry. I did not hit anyone. I did not cut wires. I did not touch the coin."

"Who pressured you," Amelia asked.

Tamsin looked toward the aft where Bradley sat with his anger in a suit. "Do not make me say it yet," she said. "Look at him. You already know."

A soft voice came from the row behind them. Mrs. Carmichael again, quiet as a benediction that wished it did not need to be said. "He studied the line from boyhood. He did not like to share."

Amelia nodded. She could feel the threads pulling tight. She could feel how a single small tool could scratch a silver crest, could open a panel, could nick a wire to make the air speak in broken sentences. She turned the diary page toward the light and photographed it with her mind, each notch and name.

"Stay where I can see you," she said to Tamsin. "If this is a frame, we will find the frame. If it is not, I will still keep you safe."

"You cannot keep all of us safe," Tamsin said, soft and fierce, a truth, not a threat. "You are one person walking a moving aisle while the past walks behind you."

"Then help me," Amelia said. "Help me land this without a body."

Tamsin's eyes flicked to the book in her hand. She slid it inside her tote and lifted her chin.

"You do not know what you are about to start," she said.

The hum went on, same pitch, same thrum, but the words hung in the air like a new switch had been armed.

Chapter 12

Night mode laid a calm veil over the rows. The aisle lights glowed like dots on a runway map. The air held the warm scent of bread rolls that never quite cooled, a comfort that tried to cover the old chill of parchment and blood talk.

Amelia checked Lionel's monitor where the physician had settled him, aft, near the galley. The man's skin had a paper tone. On his forearm, above a pale vein, a small bruise marked a dot the size of a seed. A tiny circle with a darker center. The kind a small needle would leave.

"Any change," she asked.

The physician shook his head once. "Stable enough. Not strong."

Lionel's eyelids trembled. His lips moved. Air caught in his throat and then found a path.

"Tamsin," he said, a whisper with grit in it. Then, "Bradley." He paused. "Carmichael." The names came like stones laid in a line. He drew a thin breath. "Second coin," he said, and the words shivered the quiet. "A partner."

"Partner," Amelia said, low, as if the word might startle him back. "Can you say who."

His eyes tracked past her shoulder and fixed on a place that the plane did not carry. He sank again, slow, as if the seat had turned to silt.

Deena touched Amelia's arm. "We need to hold movement," she said. "Captain wants the cabin firm."

"Do it," Amelia said.

The seat belt sign shone a steady command. Captain Reeves spoke with the warmth of a parent and the tone of a surgeon. Please remain seated. We appreciate your cooperation. We will update you soon. The hush that followed rode on engines and breath.

Bradley stood anyway. He took two steps down the aisle and planted himself in the open space as if he paid rent there. "How long do we endure this," he said, voice pitched for neighbors more than crew. "We are crossing an ocean with a vigil held at the back like a shrine."

"Sit," Amelia said. She did not raise her voice. He turned, saw no fury in her, and found no handhold for his own.

He sat.

A whisper reached her from the center rows and made itself a thread toward the galley. Betsy again, carrying a secret as if it weighed. She slipped a paper to Amelia. A photograph, edges soft from time, four faces circled in red pencil. Three were familiar: Lionel when the skin at his jaw was still tight; a woman with Greta's features worn young; a partial profile at the edge that looked like Bradley from a business article headshot with the smile reduced to its bones. The last face wore a look of defiance and shadow. The line around it had been heavier, as if the pencil had pressed harder there, as if whoever circled it knew it mattered most and hated that fact.

"Where," Amelia asked.

"Seat pocket, row twenty-three," Betsy said. "Either left by a ghost or planted by a person with a sense of theater."

"Did anyone see you take it," Amelia asked.

"Only the snack wrapper," Betsy said. "It judged me the way plastic judges everyone."

A ripple of talk rose at mid-cabin and peaked into a crest that threatened to spill. Bradley again, no longer content with two steps. He stood and pointed at Tamsin, who had not moved from her seat, the book now closed on her lap.

"This is her storm," he said. "She has chased this fortune through libraries and old men and now through the sky. She came here to force a claim."

Tamsin stood without hurry. "I came here to meet Lionel," she said. "To ask for a process that does not involve hospital monitors. I did not write threats. I did not cut wires. I did not plant tools inside panels. You accuse because you cannot stand that the story includes more names than yours."

"Enough," Amelia said. Not a shout. She placed her body in the narrow space between them and turned her face to each in turn. "You two do not get to turn an airplane into a courtroom."

Passengers watched with still hands, eyes moving and then stopping when she caught them, some with pity, some with the interest people bring to a safe emergency. Rita clutched Nolan's arm and whispered into her sleeve, "I did not pack for this."

"You packed well," Nolan said. "You brought me."

That earned him a small grin, the kind that could keep a night together.

Mrs. Carmichael raised a finger again, that old classroom reflex. "Ms. Hart," she said. "I told you I knew things. I have another piece. Years ago, Ms. Roth sent me a letter asking if I would check a registry. Mr. Gaines came to my home with a gift basket and a list of names for me to translate. He knew more than he admitted then. He was a boy when he began. He is not a boy now."

Bradley rolled his eyes toward the ceiling and sighed in a way that made other people move in their seats. Amelia did not look away from him until he looked back.

"Lionel spoke of a partner," Amelia said. "If you are not that partner, Mr. Gaines, stop acting like one."

His mouth flattened. He sat again, but the set of his shoulders said he would stand the moment a gap opened.

Greta arrived at Tamsin's row. She kept the folder hugged to her chest, the bandage at her hairline clean but a small shadow visible through the gauze. "Ms. Roth," she said. "Your line may branch, but it remains. I found proof of a branch, not a crown. If you declare a right, the old houses will answer with their own claims. We can be custodians instead of wreckers. We can put the coin where glass and a placard protect it from knives."

"You speak as if I want a throne," Tamsin said. "I want a ledger to reflect the truth. I want the word 'heir' to stop drawing blood."

Lights dimmed another notch at the captain's request. A baby gave a single cry, then decided the lullaby in the engines was enough.

Betsy's hand slipped back into Amelia's. "This photo," Betsy said. "The circles match three faces on this plane. The fourth looks like Mr. Gaines from that article you showed me on your phone at the gate. He hid a tie and pretended shock."

"Then that is our contradiction," Amelia said. "We hold it until the ground, then we put it in a police hand."

Deena leaned in from the galley. "Movement locked," she said. "Lav trips on request, escort only. Captain wants it strict."

"Good," Amelia said.

She bent to Lionel again. She could count the beats at his neck where the pulse made a small tent of skin. His eyes moved under lids as if dreams had turned to pages he could no longer keep.

"Lionel," she said. "You spoke of a second coin. Are there two tokens or a token and its partner."

His lips parted. A whisper, barely sound, came with a push of air. "Cameo," he said. "The other piece is a locket." He swallowed and winced. "Together, they lock the claim. Split, they can ruin it."

"Where," Amelia asked.

"I had it," he said. "I lost it before the dark. Someone took it. Or I gave it to the wrong hand." He took another breath that had weight. "Partner," he said again, softer. "One more hand in this. A hand that hides behind friendly words."

"Is it someone here," Amelia asked. "On this plane."

His head moved a finger width. Up, then down, as if gravity wanted both answers.

Betsy glanced down the aisle. "Ms. Hart," she said, low. "Before we boarded, Ms. Roth stood by the window and spoke three languages into her phone. She shifted between them like she flipped pages. She looked scared. Not greedy. I know the difference."

Tamsin caught the whisper even without facing them. "I have friends in Paris," she said. "Researchers. I told them I might be late. I told them I might bring trouble."

"Honesty noted," Amelia said.

The rows breathed. The hum gave back what people put into it. Fear. Hope. Want. A set of old names that did not belong to metal parts and safety cards. The faces on the photograph watched from the past with their red circles like targets or rings thrown in a fair game where the prize was a crown no one could hold.

Bradley rose again. Amelia met him before he made the third step. "Sit," she said.

"I am tired of being accused," he said. "If you have proof, show it."

"I have your name on a note in an envelope from 1982," she said, soft, so the nearest rows and he could hear but not the next cabin.

"Signed next to a woman who shares Ms. Roth's blood. You denied knowing her. You lied to me in this aisle."

He blinked once. A tell. Then he smiled in a way that pressed nothing kind into the world. He sat.

Rita whispered to Nolan, "He smiles like a paper cut."

Nolan nodded. "I like your metaphors," he said.

Lionel's hand twitched on the blanket. Amelia leaned closer, a human shape that blocked the light without casting a shadow. His mouth moved. This time the sound came with a scrape, a word dragged across a rough place and given to the air.

"Alastair," he said.

The name slid into the space like a key turning in a lock inside a wall no one had seen. Tamsin's face changed, not to triumph, more to dread and release. Mrs. Carmichael shut her eyes and nodded like a prayer she had expected to say one day and had hoped to forget. Bradley's jaw worked and then held still.

The hum went on, careful, because the airplane did not care about old vows. The airplane cared about lift and fuel and the line the pilot kept on the screen. But the name stayed, a weight that bent every story toward it.

CHAPTER THIRTEEN

Chapter 13

The cabin carried a soft hush, the kind that came after a scare and before the next one. Screens glowed. Shades half down. The engines murmured with a steady, low song that held the night together. Amelia stood in the aft galley with a stack of service napkins, the paper warm from her palm, her mind sorting threads that did not want to lie straight.

She spread Lionel's papers without showing their faces to anyone who drifted close. Betsy hovered near, ready with a grin that promised to behave, and rarely did.

"Three minutes," Betsy said. "Then I go guard the snack basket like it's crown jewels."

Amelia lifted a page from the 1980s, brittle and sweet with old dust. "Give me two," she said.

Betsy nodded. "Two, then I make coffee that can wake Paris."

Amelia traced a line of names with her eyes, a stem and its branches. Alastair de Riviere, ink pressed deep by a hand that had not spared the pen. The letter looked like a door that someone had closed without turning the handle all the way. If she could nudge it open, the rush of old air might tell her who, tonight, was breathing that same air and calling it a birthright.

She slid the list back into the folder and stepped into the aisle. The carpet kept the secrets of a thousand red-eyes and would keep this one until the wheels kissed the ground. Deena waited up the row, one hand on the cart, her eyes scanning the way Amelia had trained her eyes to scan. Row by row. Lav by lav. Not the face alone, but the body that could not hide its intent.

"Lav trips," Deena said softly as Amelia came close. "Same person keeps slipping in and out. Slight limp. Could be nothing."

"Keep time," Amelia said. "If they are meeting someone, they will be careful, but not perfect."

Deena's mouth tipped like a private joke. "No one is perfect at 3 a.m."

They moved in a rhythm learned from long nights. Smile. Check belts. Tuck a corner of a blanket beneath a chin. Pretend not to hear the whisper that was too sharp for comfort. Pass the baby aisle and let the tiny sock in the aisle be a reminder that the world still had soft edges.

The seatbelt chime sounded with a calm ping. Captain Reeves, steady as always, asked everyone to stay seated. The air felt smooth. The air did not owe them smooth.

106

A small hand reached out. Rita, eyes wide but braver now, held up two fingers. "Water?" she asked.

Amelia brought two cups. Nolan squeezed Rita's hand and thanked her as if water were a miracle. Betsy rolled the cart by, and Rita's smile won a cookie. The cookie won a mouthed thank you that made Nolan look like the luckiest man on the plane. Human warmth could live next to dread without either one choking the other.

The forward galley curtain stirred as if a breath touched it. Amelia's skin cooled. She walked, not rushed, toward the curtain, and tucked it back. Nothing but racks, tins, a coffee ring that refused to be wiped away. She eased it shut and turned.

A shiver went through the plane, a cat twitch in a dream. The overhead bins were fine, latches even. She told herself to hold her ground. The engines held theirs.

She had just reached row twenty-five when the first hard jolt hit.

Cans in the aft galley knocked into one another. A suitcase thudded from an open bin, a quick, heavy smack against the floor. A child squeaked, shocked more than hurt, then giggled at his own noise because sometimes the body chose laughter to keep from shouting.

"Everyone sit," Amelia called, her voice clear and even. "Belts tight. Heads back."

The plane bucked again. The lights kept steady, then flickered once, like a blink that lasted a beat too long. A third jolt rolled through the cabin. Somewhere, ice rattled in a cup and a straw tried to climb out.

An overhead latch gave way. A slim roller bag slid out, caught by its handle on the lip, dangled, then fell. Deena lunged and took the hit on her forearm. The bag bounced, harmless now, and she pushed it under a row with her shoe.

"Fine," Deena said, shaking her arm, the word a short breath. "Go."

Amelia knelt. Under seat 25B, something white showed, tucked back where the vacuum could not reach. She reached in and drew out a letter that smelled like it had lived in a trunk. A crease down the middle. Ink worked into the fibers. It read, in a hand that leaned forward as if it wanted to keep walking: My dearest Alastair.

She did not open it fully there. She held it against her palm long enough for her pulse to tap through it, then slipped it into her left pocket, the pocket where she kept the earlier scrap that said old score and the note that said token. The pocket where she kept the glove with A.H. stitched on the cuff. The left pocket had become a small museum.

She stood and the plane smoothed out as if it had decided enough drama for the minute. A low murmur breathed across the rows. Bradley, farther aft, dragged his hand across his face and set his jaw.

"I am done with this," he said, not to anyone, but the words hit ears. "Divert. Land. End it."

"Sir," Amelia said, "please stay seated. We will update you as we can."

He looked past her like she was a window he could not open. Tamsin, two rows up, had the worn book on her lap and her gaze on the carpet. She did not look at Bradley, not once. It told its own story.

Amelia reached row twenty-seven and stopped. The aisle felt narrower than it had five minutes earlier. She scanned left. She scanned right. She moved again.

The lights dimmed, the night setting the cabin wore like a soft coat. Captain Reeves announced they had found a smoother level. The hum steadied. For the space of two breaths, the plane felt kind.

She took the letter out in the galley and unfolded it by the sink, where the steel's faint glow gave the ink a small stage. My dearest Alastair, the letter began, I warn you as I love you, because the day we thought would set us free has put a mark on us both. If the token passes to the wrong hand, they will call it justice when they take your name from you. The rest was a tangle of hope and threat, every line a knot tied in 1982.

Betsy peered over her shoulder. "A love letter," she whispered. "Plus doom."

"Plus history," Amelia said. "The kind that does not stay in a museum."

Betsy pointed at the closing line. "She used the word vow. That matches the parchment from behind the coffee machine."

"Vow. Blood debt. Rightful heir." Amelia folded the letter and slid it back into her pocket. "It is the same song, played on different instruments."

"Less romance in blood debt, but sure," Betsy said. "Do I brew another pot?"

"Please," Amelia said. "Then circle the aft lav. Ten minutes. See if our limping friend keeps his rhythm."

Betsy gave a small two-finger salute. "You got it."

Amelia stepped into the aisle again and found Mrs. Carmichael awake, hands clasped around the strap of her bag. The older woman watched the cabin with the gaze of a teacher who knew which child had cheated on a test three rows back before the rest of the room suspected.

"Are you all right?" Amelia asked.

"I taught a boy who told lies so often that when a truth came, it could not survive in his mouth." Mrs. Carmichael's voice had a dry music. "I hear that boy every time that man talks." She nodded toward Bradley.

"Drink some water," Amelia said, and the older woman's smile said she recognized care when it came in simple cups.

Amelia moved on. She counted seconds between lav door clicks and footfalls, the metronome of a hunt that tried to look like a walk. She let the flow carry her to the forward galley curtain and stopped there a moment to listen. Metal against metal in the racks. A faint hiss from a kettle that had been shut off but still spoke. Under that, something low, like a whisper that was not a person.

She eased the curtain, stepped through, and found no one. She turned, ready to step back out.

A hand closed around her left wrist.

The grip came from the dark just outside the curtain, a quick snatch that found bone and skin. She drew in air, pulled back on instinct, and the fingers tightened. Skin pinched. Her pulse kicked.

Her other hand came up, not to strike, but to wedge between the grip and her. Whoever held her was strong, not huge, not weak, a practical strength that belonged to gym time and a need to win small battles.

She pushed her elbow against the curtain rail. The tension slackened. She yanked free. The curtain drew a line between them and then swung open. Light pooled over faces that were not the face she needed to see. People glanced up. Two eyes met hers and looked away, too fast to be guilty if guilt played by rules. It did not.

She checked her wrist. Pink skin. A thin band where the grip had pressed. She would log it later, because the body was another ledger. For now, she breathed once, then twice, slow, letting the breath drop into the same place she sent it during storms.

Deena reached her, eyes wide, voice low. "You good?"

"Fine," Amelia said. "Someone grabbed me at the curtain. Not a passenger who needed help."

Deena's mouth went tight. "Which side?"

"Right," Amelia said. "Three steps from the bulkhead."

"Then we know where they stand when they do not sit," Deena said.

"Tell Captain," Amelia said. "Note the time."

She moved again because that was the only choice. Through the rows, past sleeping heads and open mouths and slack hands that looked like the hands of people at peace. She wished peace on them like a prayer she did not say out loud.

When she passed Bradley's row, he turned in his seat and spoke without looking at her. "I want off this plane," he said.

"So do we all," she said. "In Paris."

He laughed, no humor in it, just a sound like metal scraped.

At row twenty-four she paused. 24C, the seat they had not pinned to a name when the night began to knot itself. A jacket lay across the cushion. The pocket bulged. She did not touch it. She looked for the face that carried that jacket, and did not see it.

Tamsin was across the aisle, her eyes on a page she was not reading. A pencil marked a line that had nothing to do with the text. She glanced up, then looked down.

Amelia turned toward the front to check Lionel. The physician had him propped, a blanket up to his chest, oxygen lines clear, pulse steady on the clip. The man gave Amelia a nod that told her he had done all he could do, and the body would do the rest if it wanted to live.

The plane gave a small shimmy. Not hard. Enough to remind them that they were in the sky and the sky did not belong to them. Amelia set her palm on the galley counter for a beat, felt steel under skin, then pushed off.

Betsy met her halfway with a report. "Limp is back," she said. "Lav visits at nine minutes, then seven, then nine again. Taller than me. Hoodie. Keeps the hood low like the cabin is a rainstorm."

"Good," Amelia said. "Not the hoodie, the watch. Keep it going."

"Coffee is hot," Betsy said. "So am I, but only on the inside. Do not print that on a mug."

Amelia smiled, small and grateful. She carried two cups forward, because ordinary tasks tied them to a line that would not break. At

Lionel's side she set one on the armrest for the doctor and one for Deena, who had drifted there on silent feet.

Lionel's eyelids fluttered. His lips moved, then shaped a word without sound. He swallowed. The second try made a sound.

"Partner," he whispered. "Do not trust the friend who arrives with answers."

Amelia leaned close but did not touch him. "Rest," she said. "We will keep you safe."

He shut his eyes. The skin at his temples eased, then pulled tight again.

Amelia stepped back. The captain's voice came over the speaker, a calm thread through cloth. "We expect smoother air for a stretch. Please keep your belts fastened. Cabin crew, continue as able."

She turned to go and the lights went out.

It was not a failure that fell to black and stayed there. It was a blink that held, a darkness that reached and drew a finger down the spine of the plane. A soft, collective intake passed from row to row. In that breath, a voice spoke very near her ear, but not at her ear. It carried from a speaker that should not have been live.

"You cannot protect them all."

Static. A click. The system cut clean.

Gasps. The shuffle of hands to call buttons. Amelia lifted her palms to shoulder height, the human sign for stillness. "We are here," she said. "Stay seated. We are here."

The lights returned. People blinked and it looked like relief, but relief had not been earned yet. Deena's gaze met hers and held a question.

"Intercom?" Deena asked.

"Cross check the panel," Amelia said. "Loose, frayed, tampered, any of it. Then call me."

She walked to the forward bulkhead and pressed her wrist against the cool wall for one second. Her skin stung where the hand had closed. She thought of the letter in her pocket, the word vow drawn so it could not be mistaken for any other word. She thought of the glove with A.H., stitched by a patient needle. She thought of the face she could not yet place, moving inside the blur of the cabin like a salmon in a river, pushing against the current the same as all the others, but with a purpose that sharpened the flow.

When she lifted her hand from the wall, the sting remained, a neat, pink band. She logged the time in her head. She logged the pulse of the cabin. She looked down the aisle, and the plane looked back at her, narrow and full and alive.

She started again.

A call light pinged mid-cabin. Betsy reached before Amelia did and gave the passenger what she needed, which was water for a dry throat and a word that sent fear back to its seat.

Amelia reached the aft galley and checked the service door handle by habit. The latch was firm. The gasket line clean. A faint breeze moved from the vent, cool and simple. She opened a drawer and found only spoons.

Deena checked in by interphone. "Forward panel looks normal," she said. "No loose wires I can see."

"Good," Amelia said. "We still got a voice on our line. We will note the time and wait for it to try again."

"Why do they always think the intercom is a stage?" Deena asked.

"Because it is," Amelia said. "A small one. A loud one."

"Copy," Deena said.

Amelia hung up and stared at the drawer for a long breath. Then she went to the water boiler and lifted the carafe lid to check the level. Her reflection bent in the curve of the steel. Her face looked like a person who would finish this night upright.

Betsy tapped the counter. "You did not jump when the voice hit," she said. "That is why we follow you."

Amelia shook her head. "You follow the rules. I only point at them."

Betsy lifted a brow. "Do not be humble on my time."

A laugh caught at the edge of Amelia's mouth. She let it go then pulled it back in, because the intercom could bloom again without warning. She set the carafe down and turned to the aisle.

Row twenty-five waited, because the letter had waited there for forty years and had chosen now to climb into the light. She passed each row like a checkpoint. She did not look for guilt on faces; she looked for the flinch that came when a hand remembered it had touched something it should not have.

As she reached the row, the child who had squeaked earlier snored once, a single adorable trumpet that made two people smile who did not think they could manage it. The plane accepted the sound and carried it like a small charm.

She slid the letter out once more, just enough to see the closing. It did not add names, only a plea: Do not trust the obvious ally.

Do not let him speak for you. The ink had feathered where the pen pressed too hard. The signature had been cut away, a corner torn, diagonal, the same hand that had torn another corner she had found in the jet bridge.

She slid it back, shut her eyes a second, and saw a face she could not fix yet, hovering at the edge of her mind like a photograph that belonged to someone else's album.

She opened her eyes and moved again.

The night held. No fresh jolt. The bins stayed shut. The air kept its calm shape. Somewhere down the row, Bradley shifted in his seat and craned his neck to look at Tamsin without turning his body. The movement looked petty and human. Petty and human could still kill.

Mrs. Carmichael had closed her eyes. Her hands folded, a picture of peace that did not match the history she carried in her head. The older woman's bag sat at her feet, the strap looped around her ankle in a little trick seasoned travelers used to warn a thief.

Amelia touched the back of a seat to steady her own thinking. She would carry the letter to Greta when she could get the historian alone in a light that made words clear. She would keep the cabin calm for one more hour, then one more, until the signs along the aisle turned from red to green to the soft white of arrival.

The intercom stayed quiet. It had taken its swing and had not landed a blow. Not yet.

She walked back to the forward galley and, before the curtain, she paused and looked right, three steps from the bulkhead, at the place where the hand had reached. No one stood there. The air smelled of coffee and the almond cookie that had cracked in half during the last jolt. She let the smell in and let it be a note of ordinary life.

Behind the curtain the steel gleamed. On the counter, a napkin held a ring left by a cup she had set down without thinking. In the ring, a small bead of water swam like a tiny world. She pressed the napkin flat and picked it up. The ring stayed on the steel, ghosted.

The phone chimed. Deena's voice again. "Captain says a cleaner ride for the next stretch. He wants us to keep our normal pattern, but keep eyes up near the cockpit corridor."

"Copy," Amelia said. "Tell him we had a voice on the PA during the last flicker."

"I did," Deena said. "He is not happy."

"Good," Amelia said. "Neither am I."

She hung up and stood in the space between the galley and the aisle, where the world narrowed enough to force a choice. Then she stepped into the aisle and chose to keep moving.

The hum of the engines stayed true. The rows softened, then sharpened, then softened again as eyes closed and opened. Fear did not fill the plane; it ran down the seams like a thin thread. She would not let it pull anything apart.

When she reached row twenty-five this last time, she touched her wrist and felt the small heat where the grip had been. Then she looked at the faces in that row and found one gaze already on her. The person looked away. That look would matter later. Tonight, it joined the ledger with the rest.

A minute passed. Then two. Then a little more. She could trust minutes. They did not lie, even when people did.

Somewhere aft, Betsy's whisper reached her, thin but cheerful. "Coffee that can wake Paris," Betsy said. A passenger laughed once, soft. The sound traveled forward like a moth.

The lights stayed on. The bins stayed closed. The plane held steady, and the night went still, braced for the next move that would try to take the ground from under them.

"Keep your belts fastened," Amelia said as she walked. "We will be through this soon."

She believed it as she said it. She made herself believe it the way you believed a promise you would build piece by piece. The letter pressed against her thigh. A vow lived on the page. Her own lived in her bones.

The voice did not speak again. Not then. The silence that followed it hovered, and it was not empty. It watched.

She kept walking.

CHAPTER FOURTEEN

Chapter 14

W hen the sky found a calm tier and stayed there, passengers exhaled. The screens went back to their movies, lines of light in faces that looked softer now. The engines kept their steady song. Amelia stood with Greta at the forward galley where the light had a clean honesty, and she laid the night's salvage on a tray: the single glove with A.H. stitched in dark thread, the first torn scrap at the gate, the note from under a seat that carried the same hand, the letter to Alastair from 1982, the photograph of Lionel with a stern older man, the parchment from the coffee machine gap, the diary page with the branching line that led to Tamsin and then to questions.

Greta's head carried a white bandage that made her eyes look larger. Fatigue had seated itself at the corners of her mouth, stubborn and quiet.

"Memory is a poor witness," Greta said, "but sometimes it will point."

"Point now," Amelia said.

Greta tapped the parchment and then the diary page. "The de Riviere line was not clean. It rarely is. A cousin vanished in a scandal in the early eighties. That would be Alastair. Records claimed a death at sea. I never believed those documents. Too tidy for a family that thrived on mess."

"Alastair," Amelia said. "Lionel gasped the name."

Greta lifted the glove. "A.H.," she said. "Stitching looks older than a month or a fashion whim. Could be Alastair Hughes, if he ever used that alias during the time he did dealings with the Hughes branch. Or it could be a red herring wearing pleasant thread."

Amelia held the glove's weight and felt the absent hand inside it. She set it down and glanced aft. Betsy stood guard over the snack cart like a sentry posted at a border no one could cross without permission.

"Let's line the phrases," Amelia said. "Old score. Token. Family debt. Blood debt. Vow. Rightful heir. Keep them on one page and see how they sing to each other."

Greta took the napkin and wrote the words in a column, ink neat, pressure controlled. "Language maps motive," she said.

"Who uses these phrases with comfort? A historian? A claimant? A grifter who practiced in a mirror? It matters."

Deena slipped in, eyes alert, voice even. "Safety plan," she said. "Lionel stays aft with eyes on him at all times. Greta stays forward with a buddy. We control both galleys. Lav visits timed and logged. No one loiters near the cockpit corridor. If someone tries, we redirect with calm and a tray full of pretzels. No heroics, only good habits."

Amelia nodded. "Good," she said. "We make this a bus route with rules."

"I prefer trains for romance," Deena said, and her grin came and went. "But buses keep to schedules."

"Keep to this one," Amelia said.

They moved like a team that had worked storms before. Betsy rotated to forward. Deena took a spin through the cabin, her smile as real as the steel she knew how to grip. Captain Reeves kept up his rhythm of brief announcements, steady notes laid into the night's measure.

The honeymooners raised their hands when Amelia passed. Nolan spoke first. "We need to tell you something," he said, nervous and earnest.

Rita nodded. "We overheard Ms. Roth earlier," she said. "Before all the madness. She said Bradley's name like she knew him before the flight. 'He will not answer me,' she said. Then she saw us, and she stopped."

Nolan lifted his hands. "We were not snooping," he said. "We were hunting a place for my wife's bag. I thought it was a closet. It was not."

"You did fine," Amelia said. "Thank you."

Rita looked like she wanted to help more, to fix it all with kind eyes and a good heart. Amelia wanted to believe a good heart could be proof. It was proof of character. It was not proof of innocence. She gave Rita a smile that said, I see you.

She moved on. Bradley sat with his knees wide like a man who wants to take more than his share of space. He kept his chin high, his mouth set. The posture did not argue the case he wanted it to argue.

"Mr. Gaines," Amelia said, "do you need water?"

"I need a lawyer," he said.

"Paris will have many," she said. "Choose one with a calm voice."

He did not laugh. He looked at her and then looked away, the same way a man looked away from a mirror when it showed him a hair out of place he could not smooth.

She reached Tamsin next. Tamsin had the worn book again, but her eyes were not inside it. They were on the window, where a smear of moon showed in the black. She shut the book without marking the place.

"You spoke to Bradley before boarding," Amelia said, low. "Someone overheard you say his name."

Tamsin's lips pressed together. "We had business," she said. "Not friendship. He wanted access to archival records that I have by right of my grandmother's work. He wanted shortcuts. I do not give shortcuts."

"Did he know you would be on this flight?" Amelia asked.

"I told him," Tamsin said. "I did not want him cornering me in a street in London. I prefer corners with witnesses."

"You have them," Amelia said. "All around you."

"Witnesses can be blind," Tamsin said. She looked down at her hands, knuckles pale, then unclenched them and looked up. "I did not sabotage anything. I did not attack anyone. I want what belongs to my family, but I will not take it with fear."

"Good," Amelia said. "Hold to that. It will matter."

Tamsin breathed out. The breath did not carry relief. It carried resolve.

In the forward galley, Greta tapped the photograph found earlier, the one where Lionel stood beside a stern older man. "Same jaw line as the 'Alastair 1965' image," Greta said, "though the ages do not match, of course. Family resemblances echo in odd ways."

"Patterns repeat," Amelia said, and the phrase made her think of how she had started to keep a quiet list of repeated gestures and repeated words, a way to spot a trick seen twice with different names.

Greta pulled the 1982 envelope toward her and eased a folded slip from the bottom. Ink on cream. Folded once, then again, small to hide, then again, smaller still. She opened it with care that made the paper sigh.

The note carried two names in a hand that pressed and lifted at the wrong times, the way a hand does when it is excited and wants to outrun itself. A scrawl that said the meeting had been arranged. A promise that one of them would deliver documents and the other would deliver money. The line that mattered sat at the bottom, where signatures waited.

Greta looked up. "Do not gasp," she said. "Gasping brings a crowd."

Amelia did not gasp. She took in the names like a swallow that knows the shape of water. The first signature carried flourish and certainty: the grandmother whose name had threaded through Tamsin's family stories. The second signature carried a full name she had heard spoken by a man who had denied knowing the family at all. Bradley Gaines. The paper smelled like a drawer that had stayed shut for years. It smelled like proof.

Deena slid in from the aisle and saw the names without being told. "So mister 'I do not know her' tied himself to her family forty years ago," she said. "Money on the table. Paper on the table. Great combination."

"Bradley is clever with public scenes," Amelia said. "He throws noise like a magician throws scarves. Under the scarves, he has been moving his pieces into place since before most of this cabin was born."

"Do we show him this now?" Deena asked.

"Not yet," Amelia said. "We put it in the captain's safe. Then we wait for the next move and present it when the plane can handle the air that will come with it."

Greta touched the note like a blessing. "It is a clean contradiction," she said. "The kind juries like."

They secured the paper. Amelia watched Greta's hands shake a little as the historian closed the envelope and passed it to her. The bandage at Greta's temple looked stark in this light, but her eyes were bright.

"Food and water cure many ills," Greta said. "I prescribe crackers."

"Sold out of crackers," Deena said. "Pretzels and peanuts only."

"Pretzels then," Greta said. "I will grind them between my teeth like the bones of my enemies."

Amelia laughed and it came easy for a moment. Betsy appeared as if called by laughter and set a paper cup on the counter. "Caffeine for scholars," she said.

Greta took the cup and sighed in thanks. The cup steamed. The steam wrote a tiny script in the air and vanished.

The cabin kept its gentle sway as the plane moved through a layer of air that did not mind sharing space. Amelia walked the aisle again, her steps quiet. She checked Lionel. He breathed without fight. The physician gave her a nod and a thumb pointed half up, which meant we are not worse and maybe a hair better. That counted.

Mrs. Carmichael opened her eyes as Amelia passed, and their blue steadied on her. "You found something," the older woman said.

"We found contradictions," Amelia said. "They are useful."

"In my day," Mrs. Carmichael said, "contradictions meant detention."

"In my day," Amelia said, "they mean handcuffs."

Mrs. Carmichael's smile was small, but it was there.

At row twenty-six, two men whispered with heads close. The word rightful slipped out of their huddle and into the aisle where words always wandered. Amelia let them have their conspiracy and kept going. She would not stop every rumor; she would steer the river so it did not cut a new channel through the middle of the cabin.

Deena circled back with a quiet update. "We posted near the cockpit corridor," she said. "No one loiters now. A scarf that matches Greta's was found earlier, you remember. I keep seeing the color in the corner of my eye. Old trick of the mind."

"Note it," Amelia said. "Everything is a breadcrumb until it is not."

"We will run out of bread," Deena said.

"We will be in Paris by then," Amelia said. "We will buy more."

Betsy slid a trash bag down an aisle and accepted candy wrappers like confessions. A baby slept with his hands up beside his ears, a pose that said surrender to nothing but dreams. The plane glowed with small screens and dozing faces and the quiet faith that metal and math and human attention would carry them across a black sheet of ocean.

Amelia returned to the forward galley, took a breath that reached her feet, and let it go. Greta had lined the phrases on the napkin and drawn lines between them like a teacher with string on a corkboard.

"Blood debt connects to vow," Greta said. "Vow connects to rightful heir. Rightful heir connects to token, which connects to old score. All five cluster around Alastair."

"Which means Alastair sits at the center of the wheel," Amelia said. "Or his ghost does. Or his son."

"Or a lie," Greta said. "Lies can sit in the center and make everyone else spin."

Amelia looked at the clock face above the galley door. Time had its own hum. She felt a calm she did not trust yet, but would accept. "We rest the cabin," she said. "We keep watch. When the next shake comes, we meet it on our feet."

Deena nodded and left. Greta sipped her coffee. Betsy tucked the napkin under the corner of a tray so the words would not blow away if someone opened a door to the world, which they could not do at this height, but the mind liked tidy gestures.

The minutes unspooled. The plane stayed kind. Amelia made another pass, because passes were the work and the work kept people alive. Bradley glanced up and then down, his jaw working. Tamsin sat with her book open, her gaze on her hands. Rita slept with her cheek on Nolan's shoulder. Mrs. Carmichael watched the aisle like a woman reading scripture. Lionel slept and his chest rose and fell like the sea that rolled under them.

Amelia reached the aft galley, checked the door handle, glanced at the service panels, and turned back toward the front. She carried the envelope with the signed note close to her rib cage. When she reached the forward galley again, she set it on the counter for one second to wipe a ring of water from the steel.

She lifted the envelope, and in that second of lift, something square and thin slid from the outer pocket of the envelope and skated across the steel before catching on the lip. She caught it. A small photograph. Four faces. Circles drawn with a sober pen. Three we knew. The fourth, in profile, looked like a younger Bradley with less hair and more hope. The circle around him was firm, dark. Someone had wanted to be sure no one missed that face.

"Bradley cannot deny this one," Greta said, leaning in. "Magazine profile or not, the cheekbone speaks."

"He will try," Amelia said.

"He will fail," Greta said.

"Soon," Amelia said.

"Soon," Greta said.

They slid the photograph back under the flap of the envelope and sealed that flap with a piece of tape so dull it would not tempt a thief. The tape made a small tear sound that felt like progress.

The cabin held. No flicker. No voice on the intercom. The world felt like a hallway that would lead them out. Amelia knew better than to trust hallways, but she allowed the thought to sit in the chair next to her. She did not offer it coffee.

Betsy reappeared with a slice of micro-humor that arrived like a fresh roll out of a cart. "Passenger in 31C asked if our pretzels are gluten free," she said. "I said they are plot free. He said that is my favorite kind."

Amelia's smile landed. "We will serve him a plot at landing," she said.

"Charge him extra," Betsy said, and moved on.

Greta's eyes had found another thread, the kind that lurks in the corner and raises its hand when it wants to be called on. "The diary page," she said, pointing. "Look at the margin. A modern pen added a note. 'A. de Riviere,' in a hand that does not match the old lines. Someone writes themselves back into history."

"We will need to show that to the captain when we land," Amelia said. "For now, we guard it. We guard you."

Greta dipped her head. "I do not love being guarded," she said. "I am grateful for it."

"We do not love guarding," Amelia said. "We are grateful for purpose."

Greta studied her. "You always wanted this job?" she asked.

"I wanted to see people as they are when they think no one is keeping score," Amelia said. "Planes are good for that."

Greta smiled, barely there. "You will write a book," she said.

"I will pour coffee," Amelia said. "And keep people safe."

The minute hand ticked. Somewhere aft a throat cleared. A shoe squeaked. A chuckle rose and fell. The night felt almost ordinary.

Amelia lifted the envelope again and slid it into a secure pouch at the captain's request. She logged the transfer, the time, the hands. Deena signed her name as witness with a pen that had eaten half its ink. Betsy signed with a heart beside her name and then scratched the heart out and drew a square, embarrassed at her own flourish. The square looked like a tiny window that let air into a story that needed it.

Then Amelia stepped into the aisle for another pass.

At row twenty-two, Nolan opened one eye. "We good?" he asked.

"We are steady," Amelia said.

"I will take steady," he said, and closed the eye.

At row twenty-four, the jacket in 24C had moved. Its pocket bulged less. She marked it and kept walking. The jacket's owner was still not in the seat. She logged the absence. Rows had memories if you taught them.

At row twenty-seven, Bradley turned toward the aisle as if he had felt her coming. "Are you going to claim I knew Tamsin's grandmother?" he asked, too loud.

"I do not claim things," Amelia said. "I show them."

"Show me then," he said.

"Soon," she said, and kept moving, because the moment that did the most good would not be in a heated aisle with tired eyes all around.

She reached the forward galley, met Greta's gaze, and held up the envelope, now sealed, stored, logged. Greta nodded, careful and sure.

The plane glided. The ocean below did what oceans do in the night, which is keep its secrets and cradle the light of distant ships like a choir hum under the melody of an engine. Amelia set her hand on the counter and looked down the aisle. Somewhere in that string of lights sat a contradiction that would not survive the morning.

She closed her fingers, not in a fist, but in a promise of action. Then she opened them again. The moment waited, quiet and taut.

CHAPTER FIFTEEN

Chapter 15

Night pressed against the windows, a slow quilt of cloud over ocean. Cabin lights made a low river across the aisle. The air tasted like coffee and warm plastic. One soft chime slipped down the ceiling, an electronic birdcall with no nest to fly back to.

Amelia set a folded letter on the cart's towel and rolled to Bradley's row.

"You signed in 1982 with her grandmother. Explain the signature."

Bradley stared at the letter as if it might lick him. His jaw set. The muscles at the hinge rolled like small stones under skin.

"It was family correspondence," he said.

The paper showed the weight of years. Creases like old scars, a faint ring of something once spilled in a careful hand. The ink had bled into the fibers, not a drop more.

"Her grandmother and you," she said. "Harmless note, or agreement about a claim."

He showed his smile for boardrooms, the one that glossed over trouble with words like future and synergy. The smile broke fast.

"I know Tamsin," he said. "Not well. Enough to understand. She is Alastair's granddaughter. I partnered with her for a time and then I ended it. She pushed too far."

Betsy leaned into the aisle from two rows back, eyes growing. "If this turns into a family reunion, can I hand out peanuts as party favors?"

A few tired faces eased. One honeymooner lifted a thumb as if to say keep the jokes coming. The humor fell away as another chime walked the length of the cabin, followed by the captain's voice.

"Ladies and gentlemen, we have a caution on a hydraulic sensor. Please return to your seats and fasten seat belts. Flight crew, take your stations."

Seat backs clicked. A baby murmured and found comfort against a shoulder.

Amelia slid the letter into a plastic sleeve and locked the cart brake. She met Tamsin in the aisle. The woman carried a book with crackled spine and restless edges. Her gaze had the set of a chess player who disliked the board she had been given.

"Ms. Roth," Amelia said. "Will you consent to a search of your carry on. It may help settle suspicions."

Tamsin stood very still. The book pressed to her ribs like a shield. "I want to clear my name," she said. "I am not the one tearing at your plane."

Deena joined them with a nod. They stepped to the galley curtain, then to the open space by row twenty. Passengers watched without words.

Tamsin set the bag on the jumpseat and unzipped it herself. Clothing folded with care. A notebook that carried the smell of dust and ink. A flat envelope of photos in a brittle sleeve.

"Handle them," Tamsin said. "Please do not crease."

Deena lifted the envelope and slid out a stack. One black-and-white image rested on top. Four people at a summer table. Wide collars. Hair with the shine of youth and oil. At the edge of the picture a man's profile turned toward light, strong cheekbone and nose like a blade that someone had filed shorter. On the back, in clean block letters, a label: Alastair—1965.

"Where did you get these," Amelia asked.

"From a family contact in Lyon," Tamsin said. "I sought proof. Not theater. I will not forge blood."

Another chime cut across them. The captain again, steady as a metronome.

"We are evaluating. If the caution persists, we will divert to the nearest field. We are in contact with operations. Remain seated."

The hush after an announcement had a strange gravity. It pulled people into themselves. Amelia looked back to Bradley. He watched Tamsin's photos with the hunger of someone who believed paper might transform into cash if stared at long enough.

"Why lie about 1982," she asked him.

"I did not lie," he said. "I minimized. What would you have me do. Deliver a lecture on all our sins. This is a flight, not a court."

"You signed your full name," she said.

"It was a courtesy."

"Courtesies bind people."

He tried the smile again and found no traction. The corners of his mouth held for a breath, then fell.

Betsy drifted toward the aft galley with a trash bag in one hand. Her voice dropped to a whisper near Amelia's shoulder.

"I caught a shape by the rear hatch," she said. "Same jacket as earlier when the panel gave us trouble. The one with the frayed cuff."

"Where."

"Thirty rows back and then gone."

Amelia set the photos back in the envelope and gave it to Tamsin. "Thank you. Keep them close."

She moved down the aisle, passing the sleeping and the pretend-sleeping. The floor pulses came up through her shoes, tiny messages from a machine that had become most of the world they could use tonight. Trash blinked from cupholders. A magazine lay open to a beach none of them would see until morning.

At the rear service door, the trim panel showed a smear of something like graphite at the edge. Not a handprint. A brush of contact. She bent and traced the frame with her eyes. No gap large enough for a finger. No evidence to haul to the cockpit. Only that smear, as if a machine had kissed the door and left a mark.

She stood and looked back up the long room. So many faces. Some hopeful. Some carved with the old carefulness that comes from loss. She let the tension draw into a point inside her chest, and she chose what to do with it.

"If we do not stop them, we will not land safe."

Her voice was not loud. Deena heard her anyway and nodded once.

A call light came alive three rows over. A hand rose and fell. The chime spoke again, then stopped, as if thinking about the next word.

"You should sit," said the physician from the last row. "Or at least brace. That caution light is not a story you want to ignore."

Amelia gave him a small smile that did not sell anything. "Thank you, doctor. We are working it."

A fresh hiss from a soda can on the cart near Betsy made a bright note in the quiet. Betsy lifted the can and mouthed sorry. The honeymooners gripped each other's fingers and let out the tiniest laugh. Life insisted on itself in silly places.

Bradley stood halfway, then sank back down when Amelia looked at him.

"You will not pin this on me," he said.

"No one is pinning," she said. "We are aligning facts."

"They never land," he said. "Facts. They drift. That is the trouble. You catch one with your pretty stewardess hands, and another floats by like a balloon."

She did not answer. His words had added heat and no light. She returned to Tamsin.

"The label on the photo," she said. "Who wrote it."

"My grandmother," Tamsin said. "She loved ink on paper. She hated phones."

"How sure are you about the man."

"Not sure at all," Tamsin said. "It could be a cousin. It could be a lie told to her before I was born."

"Then why carry it."

"Because it feels like a string," she said. "Pull the right one and a knot opens."

The captain called Amelia on the interphone. "We are stable for now," he said. "Continue service only as safety allows. I want eyes on the rear area."

"We have them," she said. "One smear at the hatch. Nothing more."

"Copy. Bring me anything solid. Keep tempers down."

She hung up and breathed through her nose. The coffee odor was stronger near the galley. It mingled with the clean bite of disinfectant and the salt ghost of old meals. She gathered cups and wrappers, small tasks that calmed passengers who needed to see hands moving.

Betsy brushed past again, whisper thin. "He is back there," she said. "Not Bradley. Taller. Same jacket. Head down. He knows how to be a shadow."

"Stay near me," Amelia said.

They did not chase him. They tended to their people and kept watch. The aisle settled into short nods and small thanks. That was the work inside a tube at altitude. See everything. Let nothing grow wild. All the while, pray the machine over their heads kept its own counsel.

Bradley's eyes slid to the rear one more time. His mouth twitched. If guilt had a smell, it would be metal and heat.

"Mr. Gaines," Amelia said, "if you need to walk, wait for the seat belt sign to go off."

"I am fine," he said.

"Good."

The sign stayed on. The ocean stayed patient. The smear on the hatch dried into the idea of a fingerprint and nothing more. The strange night found a low gear and held it.

Deena came back from a check and set one palm flat on the jumpseat cushion. "I do not like this," she said. "Something is teaching itself how our cabin works."

"We will teach it something back," Amelia said.

"You like that," Betsy said with a small grin. "You sounded like a movie trailer."

"I sounded tired," Amelia said.

The next chime did not come with an announcement. It came like a small heart that refused to quit, quick and stubborn. Somewhere in the cabin a child said I want to be on the ground. Somewhere else a man kissed a rosary and shut his eyes as if sleep were a door he could choose.

Amelia checked the photos one more time and handed them back. "Keep them in your sight," she said.

"I will," Tamsin said.

Amelia slid the letter sleeve deeper into her pocket. The plastic rasped her knuckles. She turned toward the rear, watched the seam of the hatch, then lifted her chin and took in the whole field. The night at the windows was still that same piece of cloth, stitched with the faint pulse of stars. The engine hum pressed a steady hand against ribs and spine. She felt like a guard in a museum no one had known they were visiting. Paintings hung everywhere. Most had the same title. Family.

She rolled the cart forward and met the aisle with her shoulders square.

"Eyes up," she said to Deena. "We work. We watch. We land."

Deena gave a single nod. Betsy saluted with two fingers and then pretended never to have done it. The honeymooners shared a smile that said this was not the story they had bought tickets for, but it would be one they would tell.

From the back, a soft scrape, then silence.

Amelia kept moving.

CHAPTER SIXTEEN

Chapter 16

The hum evened out and spread like a long breath over metal and cloth. The chime stayed silent. For a moment, the plane felt like a house again, a long narrow house with soft walls and strangers who had become neighbors by need.

The captain's voice came without strain. "We have the caution contained. Crew, continue with heightened awareness. We are stable."

Amelia and Deena moved to the rear corridor. A service panel sat proud of the wall by the access frame, not enough to trouble a passerby, enough to bother a crew member with a habit of straight lines. The frame seam wore a new nick that caught the light.

"See it," Deena said.

"I do."

Amelia slid her fingers along the edge and found a latch that had not settled. She lifted and eased the panel back. Inside, a bundle of sensor lines showed a small plastic device clipped with the care of a thief who liked tidy work. A thin strip of tape held the thing in place where no tape was meant to live.

She did not touch the wires. She did not pull the tape. She looked until she could build a picture strong enough to carry in her head. A notch on the device had a bite pattern, two little triangles, like teeth on the wrong animal. She had seen those edges on the coin when it came back to them, faint gouges in a tight ring. She had seen a similar cut at the tampered panel up front.

"Captain," she said into the interphone. "We have a device at the rear access. It is taped to the bundle. We will not disturb it without you."

"Hold position," he said. "I am coming."

He arrived with the co-pilot, both with eyes that looked at problems the way surgeons look at tumors. Precise. Curious. Determined to remove.

"Good catch," he said.

He gloved up, cut the tape with a cutter from his pocket, and lifted the device with the gentlest pinch at its sides. He set it in a meal container, closed the lid, and handed it to the co-pilot.

"We keep it for evidence," he said.

Amelia pointed at the notch. "Those teeth match marks we have seen. The coin wore them after it reappeared. The forward panel too."

"Then our person brings their own kit," he said. "Thank you."

He turned to go, then faced them again. "You two keep doing what you do. The rest of us will keep the sky where it belongs."

They smiled for a heartbeat at that and then the cabin folded back over them.

Near the last row, Lionel shifted on the makeshift stretcher. The physician kept a hand on his shoulder. Lionel's eyes opened to slits, each eye a glass door with frost on it. He looked past Amelia at a point that had more weight than the room.

"Water," the physician said.

Amelia held a cup to Lionel's mouth. He swallowed. The sound was small and human.

Lionel lifted a shaking finger toward the photo Deena had tucked in the seat pocket. The one marked with the name from a different century. The name that refused to die.

"He is here," Lionel whispered. "Name changed. Face the same."

The words threw a new net across the cabin. People leaned without knowing they leaned. The air cooler whispered above them, a white noise that made secrets feel like rain behind a wall.

"Rest," the physician said.

Lionel closed his eyes. His hand sought the blanket and found it. The shaking faded.

Amelia studied the photo again. The man in profile. The cheekbone that cast a narrow shadow. The particular slope where nose met brow. She let the picture sit in her head and then she looked around the cabin, not with a scan, but with the kind of seeing that settles and waits.

Harold, the quiet man in 32D, watched the scene with a tired grief. Bradley, five rows forward, pinched the bridge of his nose. Tamsin did not blink. Greta's mouth pressed to a line as she sorted names and lines and old house trees that had thrown ugly roots.

Greta approached with her folder hugged to her ribs. The bandage over her hairline had held. Her eyes were clear now, flint and compassion in equal measure.

"I have pages that matter," she said.

They moved into the galley space by the curtain, the place where two carts slept nose to tail. Greta laid out a diagram of the family branches. Names in an old hand. Lines like creek beds cut into unbleached paper.

Tamsin took a breath and opened her notebook. Receipts for archive time stamps. Library slips. Dates that could be verified. A letter of inquiry to a French archivist with an institutional stamp in blue.

"I looked," Tamsin said. "I did not invent."

"You kept copies," Amelia said.

"I keep everything."

Greta's finger drifted along the branches. "Here is the fork where rumor insists Alastair died. Here is the cousin who took possession when no proof of him remained."

She opened another sleeve and slid out a page that did not belong with the others. The paper was bright. The ink sat on the surface like a man at the edge of a pool who has only just put his feet in. At the bottom, a clean, nervous signature: A. de Riviere.

"When did you find this," Amelia asked.

"In the mess when I went down by the cockpit," Greta said. "Papers everywhere. I thought it came from my folder. It did not. The signature is modern. The line drawn above the name has a tremor, not the old cursive clarity. The ink stayed wet on my thumb for a second."

"Tamsin," Amelia said, "does this page look like your work."

"No," Tamsin said.

Bradley stepped into the galley mouth with the photo in his hand as if it were a warrant. He lifted it, arm stiff, like he might swear on it.

"Look at him," he said. "Look at Alastair. Look at the mirror his face makes in that man back there. We have our pretender and we have our conspirator. We have our thief."

"You like messes you can point at," Greta said. "They keep your mess safe."

Bradley's mouth curled. "You believe this woman," he said to Amelia, "with her folders and stamps. She has walked this plane planting pages for hours."

Tamsin flinched and then held. Her eyes shone. She did not blink still. She had learned some years ago that blinking in front of a man like Bradley invited him to step through you.

The curtain moved near the business-class end. Only an inch. Enough to let a shoulder slip through if someone wanted to become part of their air.

"Stay with me," Amelia said to Deena without turning.

Greta tapped the diagram. "One more piece," she said. "The final piece sits with a letter I kept back because I thought it too combustible for this box of nerves."

"Get it," Amelia said.

Greta turned to her seat. She never made it there. A figure glided into the space and knocked her hard against the cart. The folder flew. Pages like winter leaves lifted and turned.

Amelia stepped in and blocked the second strike with her forearm. The attacker jerked away with cat lightness. A sleeve brushed Amelia's wrist where a faint bruise still mapped the earlier grab. A scent of machine oil and soap hung in the air. The figure vanished through the curtain and into the stream of passengers who did not know they had become cover.

"Greta," Deena said, crouching. "Can you stand."

"Yes," Greta said. "Pain but nothing broken."

Betsy appeared at the curtain with a look that could cut wire. "He went forward, then doubled back. He is hunting the center."

"Positions," Amelia said. "We work the perimeter. We pull in the papers."

They gathered the sheets. Amelia stacked the old ones into a pile that looked like it had grown up together. She set the bright sheet with the fresh signature aside. The ink had dried now. The letters were still too crisp, the way a counterfeit smile keeps every tooth visible.

"Final piece," Greta said from the jumpseat, breath short. "It sits in my notes. A receipt that shows who asked for the certified copy in Paris last month. The person used a modern alias but the address belongs to an old branch."

"We will find it," Amelia said.

Bradley paced in a small cage of his own making. He lifted the photo and jabbed it in the air. "You look at old ink and romance yourselves blind. Look at faces. That man is on this plane."

Harold stood now. His hands shook. He did not speak. The line of his nose cut the cabin light into a familiar shape. He looked like the man in the picture if you aged the paper and pressed it under books for fifty years.

"Sir," Amelia said. "Remain seated for now. We will speak as we can."

He sank down again. The eyes he lifted to her were complicated. Fear. Shame. A piece of hope that looked misplaced but refused to move.

Amelia studied the forged page again. The loop of the A had a stall in it where the pen hesitated and then pushed. A left-hander might make a line like that if forced to write in a rush against the body. The surname curve ended in a point, not a flourish. She slid the page into a clear sleeve and handed it to Deena.

"Captain should log this," she said. "Chain of custody. Then police."

Deena nodded and moved to the interphone.

Greta pressed two fingers to the bridge of her nose, then lifted her head. "You saw the device," she said.

"We did," Amelia said. "Same bite mark we saw in the scratches on the coin."

"Then the man with the kit is the man with the nerves," Greta said. "He thinks the plane is a board he can play."

"We will flip his board," Betsy said. "I mean. Politely."

"Politely," Amelia said. "Always."

The captain's voice returned. "We are good on systems. We will proceed to destination. Cabin crew, continue to monitor all areas and report any concerns immediately."

Amelia looked at the long room again. Every seat had become a square on a game that started before any of them were born. She felt the weight of her badge, a small piece of plastic that said she belonged to this space and owed it protection. Not a detective badge. Something kinder and harder at the same time.

She lifted Greta's fallen folder from the floor and slid the papers back inside, old with old, new with new. The forged page lay apart in its sleeve like a bright lie that wished it could clay-coat itself and pass as ancient.

"Someone wrote this name in our air," she said. "Someone wanted the past to speak in a present voice."

Tamsin looked at the page and shook her head. "I would rather lose the claim than win it like that."

"I believe you," Amelia said.

Bradley laughed once without humor. "You will believe anything in this mood," he said.

Amelia did not answer him. She had no time for the way he used noise to build a fog. She had a plane that needed clean paths and a story that needed clean lines.

She set Deena on the rear watch again, placed Betsy in the middle like a human radio that caught whispers from both directions, and kept Greta in sight with a cold pack on the bandage and water within reach. The physician stayed near Lionel and gave a nod like steady ground.

The night outside kept its counsel. The ocean did not judge their small war.

Amelia ran a finger over the sleeve of the forged page once more. The plastic bumped under her nail. The ink did not belong to any old hand. It belonged to this hour. To this narrow place between sky and sea.

Someone had written A. de Riviere in fresh black and expected the cabin to accept it.

Amelia looked up and let the thought stand where everyone could see it.

"Someone is forging the past on this plane."

Greta closed her eyes for a breath. Then she opened them and gave the smallest, fiercest nod. "Then we stop them," she said.

Amelia stood in the galley mouth and raised her chin toward the forward rows. The aisle ran like a thin river of light. Somewhere in that light moved a hand with a little set of tools and a plan older than anyone could carry without breaking.

She did not break.

She watched.

She waited.

She worked.

Chapter 17

The galley curtain hung motionless. Plastic cups nested in stacks, lids clicked in their trays, and the engine's low drone ran under everything like a steady drum far below the floor. Coffee scented the narrow aisle, sweet and burnt at once. Amelia kept one hand on the counter and the other on the folder they'd made to look important. The paper inside was nothing but copied lines and a crest traced in pen. It looked old from across the galley. It looked like power if you wanted it to.

A passenger coughed somewhere behind the curtain. Someone else laughed, a quick, brittle burst that broke off. Deena stood on the far side of the service cart, eyes on the corridor. Betsy dangled a trash bag like a party favor and tried to look casual. She did not pull it off.

"Do we say the line again?" Betsy whispered.

"We don't say anything," Amelia said.

Betsy nodded and made a face. "Right. Invisible. My best skill."

Another minute stretched. The aircraft ticked: tiny clicks in the ceiling panels, the air system's gentle push at her sleeve. Captain Reeves had given them three steady announcements over the last half hour: systems holding, route locked, crew at the ready. Calm words, even cadence, no extra shine. He knew how to hold a room while strapped behind a door.

The bait lay open on the counter under the night light, the title scrawled in block caps: DEFINITIVE FAMILY PROOF. Greta had smudged the edges with damp fingers until the paper developed soft gray arcs, the kind of filth that only time made. The crest had a nick at ten o'clock, to echo the coin Lionel hid and lost and found again. They'd done their work. Now the cabin would do the rest.

Footsteps softened near the curtain. Then passed. Amelia's heartbeat settled and then rose again for no reason she could state. She cataloged the pieces in her head: the coin back in play, fresh scratches on its face; wires slashed behind a loose panel hours ago; a bruise on Lionel's arm that looked like a puncture from something thin. Every item lived in one line now. If she tugged, the whole rope might move.

A couple from row twenty-three appeared at the split in the curtain. Nolan hovered at Rita's shoulder as if the fabric might bite her. He held two ginger ales. She mouthed "thank you" at Deena and, with a shy smile at the folder, asked if this was where the good cookies were kept. Deena palmed two from the drawer and sent them back with a wink. That tiny square of sweetness restored a piece of the room. Amelia watched it pass and stored the feeling where she kept all useful things.

"Wait," Betsy murmured.

The fabric lifted a thumb's width. A hand slid in, hesitated, then vanished. Not a grab; a probe.

Amelia nodded once. Deena shifted her stance, weight on the back foot. Greta, a few seats away, kept her eyes on a crossword she wasn't filling and used the pen as a pointer to the fake crest whenever anyone glanced down the aisle. Bradley had gone to ground two rows behind, hunched over his briefcase like a man bracing for a wave. Every so often he raised his head and scanned the cabin with a twitchy, righteous glare. It only made his seat mates draw their elbows closer.

Back near row twenty-nine, Mrs. Carmichael sat with her hands folded around a cup as if heat could travel through paper and give her bones more time. She'd told Amelia earlier that the token once sat in a parlor near Paris, that a servant dusted the mantel every day around it. She spoke as if she had stood in that room herself.

A cart wheel creaked. The curtain stirred. The hand returned.

It was quick—she had to give that. Fingers slipped past the slit, landed on the folder, and tugged. The paper skittered. The hand yanked again. Amelia pressed the switch on the small light clipped inside the service door and threw a clean circle of white over the counter and the thief's sleeve.

"Stop," she said.

The figure flinched and pulled hard. The folder came free. The curtain snapped on its rail. A shoulder hit the cart with a hollow thock. Trays rattled. Bottled water danced. The thief started to turn, but Betsy stepped into the gap like a shortstop and took one clumsy swipe at the paper, missed, and spun, her trash bag cracking like a flag.

Deena slid along the counter and blocked the aisle with the cart. The figure had no exit except through the light.

Amelia aimed up, not at the face yet, and raised the beam on a slow arc so the eyes would follow. She'd learned that trick in a class that had nothing to do with flying planes and everything to do with keeping people safe inside them. The light kissed a cheek, then a nose, then a mouth pinched tight. The scarf slipped.

Mrs. Carmichael squinted against the glare. For a breath she looked both older and much younger. Then the lines fell back into place. Her left hand held the folder. Her right hand held a small blade that looked born from a letter opener and a broken nail file. Shiny and sad.

"Mrs. Carmichael," Amelia said.

"I act for my family," the older woman said. Her voice carried further than Amelia expected. Heads turned up the aisle like flowers to light. "If you won't give me the proof, I'll take it."

"Set the blade down," Deena said.

Mrs. Carmichael shook her head. It was tiny, the kind of no you give a child who doesn't understand the stakes. She pivoted, clearing the cart by inches. The blade flashed once. She didn't swing.

She held it low and close, point toward the floor, like someone who knew she could be dangerous and wished she didn't have to be.

Betsy stumbled back against the side rail and caught herself with a hand on the ice bin. "She was the whisper," Betsy said, not to anyone and to everyone. "The scarf voice from the galley. She was the one."

"Move aside," Mrs. Carmichael said. "The cockpit will know what to do."

"Stop," Amelia said again. "No one goes forward."

Mrs. Carmichael's eyes flicked down the length of the cabin. She didn't look at Bradley. She didn't look at Tamsin, who sat very still with a worn book open, as if any motion might wake the worst part of the night. She looked toward Lionel, and her gaze fixed there, and something inside her set like plaster.

Greta stood slow, palms out. "We can talk here," she said. "No one needs to be brave with a knife."

"It isn't a knife," Mrs. Carmichael said. "It's a key."

"Then you won't mind setting it on the cart," Deena said. "Keys ride better when they're not in hands."

For a moment, the plane belonged to quiet noises. A soda fizzed six rows back. The baby from earlier gave a sigh that sounded like the end of a very long day. A man cleared his throat as if preparing to ask for the time and then thought better of it.

"Please," Amelia said. She softened her voice because it was the only tool she hadn't used yet. "Let's not scare anyone else. You've scared me enough for one night."

Mrs. Carmichael looked at her. The older woman's eyes filmed with something that wasn't pure rage and wasn't simple fear. Behind the film was a ledger of names, some crossed, some underlined. "You don't know the half of it," she said.

The blade twitched. The folder crinkled in her grip. Then she juked right, feinted left with a shoulder turn that would have fooled someone with less stake, and darted for the narrow seam between cart and wall.

Amelia reached. The light slipped from her hand, bounced, spun, and threw a disco of glare up the ceiling. She caught cloth, not skin. Mrs. Carmichael tore free. The folder thumped the cart. Pages fanned like startled birds. The blade flashed again, still low, still meant to warn.

"Ma'am," Captain Reeves called from behind the cockpit door, voice clear through the interphone. "Do not approach."

"I can fix this," Mrs. Carmichael said, and in that promise lived fifty years of bad deals. She lunged toward the forward corridor.

Betsy threw her trash bag like a net. It caught a shoulder and slid off, crinkling like a deflated balloon. Deena kicked the cart a foot to close the gap, metal on metal, and the aisle narrowed to a slit. The older woman planted a hand on the cart edge and vaulted—not high, not young, but committed.

Amelia stepped into her and met her at the rail. Elbow to sternum, not hard. The blade pointed away. "Please," Amelia said, breath short now. "Look at me."

For a second, they were two women in a kitchen instead of a tube in the sky. Steam rose behind them. A clock ticked. Somewhere in the past a letter lay on a table and no one reached for it in time.

"I act for my family," Mrs. Carmichael said again. She pulled the hood from her scarf. The blade turned in her hand like a conclusion.

Then she twisted free with a speed that came from a place too old to practice. She slid along the wall and bolted toward the cockpit corridor, a small figure with a paper crown in her fist and a scrap of metal that could ruin a life in the wrong angle.

"Stop her," someone said.

Amelia pushed off the cart and followed.

The floor hummed through zip ties. Plastic cut into skin. Mrs. Carmichael's chest rose against the belt crossed over her ribs. The aft galley hummed with the low conversation of a plane that had just watched a bad thing sail past a worse one. The blade lay on the counter in a napkin nest. The forged folder sat beside it under a coffee pot as if heat could shrink the lies back to size.

"We're going to give you water," Amelia said. "You'll drink. Then we'll talk."

Mrs. Carmichael nodded once, proud even in a web. She took the cup with both hands and sipped, a bird at a puddle.

Greta stood half a step behind Amelia, her pen capped for the first time in an hour. Deena hovered at the curtain, back to the room, body a door. Betsy held the trash bag tight against her side like a purse she had sworn to protect.

"What I did was necessary," Mrs. Carmichael said. She spoke to a line at the floor and nobody at all. "You think crooks latch a door and call it duty. You think duty is a uniform and a smile. But duty is a promise you can't pay off any other way."

"Who pushed you to this?" Amelia asked. "You're not alone."

A long blink. "I am alone right now," she said, and the answer was truer than the question. Then she exhaled. "No. I had letters. Years of them. I was asked to study, to fetch, to wait, to be patient. I was told the coin had to be in the right hands so the wrong line would stop bleeding the name dry. I was told that if I didn't help, other people would help and they would not use soft ways."

"Letters from whom?" Greta asked.

Mrs. Carmichael pressed her lips together. She shook her head. "From family," she said.

"Which branch?" Greta said, voice calm as a guide in a museum that had seen fires and floods and still hung every frame.

"The branch that stayed quiet the longest," Mrs. Carmichael said.

"Do you know the person's name?" Amelia asked. "The one writing to you."

"I know a letter," the older woman said. "A sign. 'A.' That was the signature. It was always the first letter and a dot, like a stamp. Sometimes it came as a card, sometimes as a page cut from a legal pad. None from a computer. Always a hand."

"How did you reach Greta?" Amelia asked.

"I didn't," Mrs. Carmichael said. "I reached a librarian in Antwerp who knew a teacher in Calais who knew a woman in

London who had a student at the Sorbonne. Greta found me because she hunts the past like it stole her watch."

Greta's mouth tightened. "I document," she said.

"And you do it well," Mrs. Carmichael said. "Better than most. That's why he feared you."

"He," Amelia said. "The author of the letters?"

The older woman looked at her cup. "He," she said.

"Alastair," Greta said.

Mrs. Carmichael did not answer. She set the cup down on the counter. Her hands looked very old on the white lid.

From the interphone came Captain Reeves's measured tone. "Cabin status steady. We remain en route. Security holds. Thank you." The words seeped down the aisle and quieted the hearts that could hear them.

Amelia remembered the blade flashing low, not to cut but to warn, and the way Mrs. Carmichael had tried to pass with the speed of someone who could not carry any more years. The pity in that thought irritated and saddened her at once.

"You were the informant," Amelia said. "In the dark galley earlier. You told me the truth would draw blood if we pulled it now."

"I told you what I was told to tell you," Mrs. Carmichael said. "Tell them to be patient. Hold the proof. Wait for the right hands. If you dug too soon, the wrong hands would start to shake." She gave a small smile without joy. "I guessed that part myself."

"Why the sabotage?" Deena asked without turning from the curtain. "Wires in a panel. A device in the back. Those things harm people who aren't on your list."

"I didn't set a device," Mrs. Carmichael said, head snapping up as if accused of theft in a church. "I distracted. I sent notes. I opened a bin. I feared the dark would make you calm. But I would not steer a plane into grief."

"Who would?" Greta said.

"The one with more to lose," Mrs. Carmichael said. "The one whose face burns when he's told no."

Bradley's voice floated from the cabin, too loud and too certain. "This is unlawful restraint," he declared to a woman in row twenty-two. She gave a small nod as if he'd asked about the weather.

Amelia folded the forged folder closed. The heat of the coffee pot had bled into the paper. She could feel it in her palms.

"What did 'A' promise?" Amelia asked.

"An end," Mrs. Carmichael said. "One quiet end instead of a hundred slow ones."

"And what did he threaten?" Greta asked.

"My job at a small school if I didn't carry one letter. Then, if I didn't help him with a list of names, he would publish things that would make a church turn its back on me. None of it the sort of thing a court would care about. All of it the sort of thing that sits on a heart and doesn't leave."

"Did you ever see him?" Amelia asked. "In person."

"No," Mrs. Carmichael said. "But I saw a photograph once. A young man by a pond with his jacket on his knees. The back said 'Alastair—1965.' It came folded in a blue airmail sleeve with the edges red and white. I kept it five days and sent it back."

Greta's pen tapped once against her wrist. "The same hand that signed the old letters in Lionel's envelope?" she asked.

"The old letters were from another century," Mrs. Carmichael said. "The ones I carried were new. The words were the same. 'Broken promise.' 'Blood debt.' He wanted a chorus so you'd know the song."

Betsy shifted from foot to foot. "I'm going to say the quiet part," she said. "We need to tell people that knives are not moving down the aisle and we have this woman here. We need to give them a cookie and a plan."

"Cookies we can do," Deena said. "Plans are Amelia's department."

Amelia drew a breath. "Here's the plan. We keep you in the aft galley with a restraint for now," she said to Mrs. Carmichael. "You'll answer questions and then we'll hand you to the people waiting at the end of the jet bridge. No one else gets to be a hero. No one else gets hurt."

Mrs. Carmichael nodded. "That part sounds right."

"Is there anything else you kept?" Amelia asked. "Anything on you right now."

The older woman hesitated. It was a small pause, but she could not sell it as noise. "Only my purse," she said.

"May I check it," Amelia said.

Mrs. Carmichael looked at the ceiling. There must have been a square she could stare into and see a field in late summer. She brought herself back down and nodded.

158

Amelia set the purse on the counter, tabled the flap, and ran practiced fingers along seams and liners. Tissues. Old ticket stubs. A comb with a missing tooth. An envelope, sealed, no stamp. Her name on it in a tidy, teachable script.

"Whose is that," Betsy breathed, already knowing.

Mrs. Carmichael stared at the envelope like it had grown there without her consent. "He told me to keep it sealed until I could place it in the hands of the person who stood up when the room asked for someone brave."

"Who is that," Greta asked softly.

Mrs. Carmichael looked at Amelia.

"Open it," Deena said.

Amelia slid a nail under the flap and lifted it without tearing the paper more than it had to be. Inside lay a single sheet. Across the center, in block letters, was a sentence that made her shoulders go cold.

Fail me, and you fail the family — A.

There was nothing else on the page. No date. No salutation. No place. The pen had dug hard enough to leave grooves where the letters turned.

Amelia held the page up to the light, then lowered it. She could feel the cabin shift. Not physically. Not yet. A collective breath had moved down the aisle as wordless rumor quickened and grew.

"Systems?" she asked into the interphone.

"Stable," Captain Reeves said. "No new messages. Keep the aisle clear."

"Copy," she said, and replaced the handset.

Greta leaned closer to the note. "Modern ink," she said. "Lines strong, no feathering. No age."

"I told you," Mrs. Carmichael said, not with triumph but with the weariness of someone who has repeated a hard line too many times. "He is not dead."

"Maybe he is a story in someone else's mouth," Greta said. "A face used like a stamp. The words fit too easily."

"He used 'A' when he taught me to fear him," Mrs. Carmichael said. "He would not share his full name. He thought that made him a wind no one could grab."

A rustle at the curtain. Rita peeked in, eyes wide, Nolan's hand anchoring her by the elbow. "Is it over?" she asked.

"For now," Deena said. "Seat belts stay on. Snacks in two minutes."

Rita exhaled and nodded. "We heard the word family and I—well, it's our honeymoon. Family sounded loaded." She blushed at her own joke, small and brave.

"Congratulations," Amelia said, and meant it like a blessing.

They withdrew. Betsy put a cookie on the counter beside the note and looked at it as if the sugar could soak up a threat.

Amelia turned back to Mrs. Carmichael. "Who else knew about this handoff," she asked. "Who else knew you had an envelope with a test in it."

"No one," the older woman said. "He gave it to me on paper to keep me from saying his name. He thought paper would make me honest."

"Paper made you nervous," Betsy said. "It makes everyone nervous on planes."

"It made me heavy," Mrs. Carmichael said. "But weight is not always a bad thing. It keeps you from floating off."

"Tell me the last letter before this one," Amelia said. "What did it demand."

"'Break the chain so the wrong heir cannot land in Paris,'" Mrs. Carmichael said. "He asked me to secure the coin by any means that did not spill blood in public. He promised that if I did not act, another would use a stronger hand."

"Another," Greta repeated. "So he has a partner."

"Or a shadow," Mrs. Carmichael said.

Bradley's argument rose again in the cabin, then fell under the Captain's calm. A buzz of private talk drifted to them, curiosity fed by the sight of belts and a woman with white hair sitting straight and tidy even when tied.

"We'll log this note," Amelia said. "We'll keep it as part of the chain. We'll tell the people waiting on the ground that you cooperated once we stopped you from rushing the front. That is the best I can do for you."

Mrs. Carmichael nodded. "You would have made a good teacher," she said. "You stand at the front and make the rules sound kind."

Amelia folded the page, slid it back into the envelope, and placed it beside the small blade, which now looked like a toy that had lost its owner. She looked at the belts around the older woman's waist and hands again and hated them and understood them at once.

"We keep going," she said to no one and to everyone. "Paris is a few hours away."

In the seats beyond the curtain the dark held steady and the hum kept time. Far back, someone chuckled at a movie. Up front, the cockpit murmured to a city on the edge of a new day. Between those poles, people slept, kept watch, or learned the limits of what they'd assumed they could bear.

Greta breathed out. "We should sort her notes," she said. "He used the same words as the old letters. That linkage matters."

"It will matter in court," Amelia said. "It matters to me now because it means we're not chasing fog."

Betsy rolled her shoulders. "Fog would be easier," she said. "Fog doesn't write threats with a dot for a name."

"Cookies in two," Deena said again, and her voice made a promise that felt almost like peace.

Amelia pressed her palm to the counter, steadying herself on something solid. The coin had left new marks when it returned. The page in her hand bore fresh grooves. People who wanted the past to win had climbed aboard at a gate, smiled at an agent, lifted bags into a bin, and sat down.

She looked at Mrs. Carmichael. "When we land," she said, "you'll tell them everything you told me. If you tell less, someone else will tell more, and you'll have lost the chance to write your own part."

"I will tell them," Mrs. Carmichael said. "But I will not say his name if it brings him to the door of a house he doesn't deserve."

"You won't have to," Amelia said. "We'll find another door."

The envelope with its short sentence lay between them. On the other side of the curtain, a plane full of lives waited and drank water and tugged blankets to their shoulders. The hum held. The night did, too.

And the letter's single initial sat on the counter like a point on a map no one wanted to visit, but every path circled anyway.

Chapter 18

The cabin lights had the hush of a chapel after the last hymn. Coffee steamed in little white clouds, and the smell of warm bread drifted up the aisle from the sealed carts like a memory of morning. The belts around Mrs. Carmichael's wrists were snug but not cruel. She sat tall, chin up, eyes steady on the seam in the galley wall as if a blackboard lived there. When she spoke, it was to the air as much as to Amelia.

"I was a teacher for thirty years," she said. "I taught boys who thought the past was a trick and girls who thought it was a mirror."

"What do you think it is," Amelia asked.

"A river," Mrs. Carmichael said. "You wade where you can stand. You don't try to drink it whole."

Amelia brought a cup of water to her, then set another on the counter for herself. "We're going to do this with care," she said. "Names, letters, instructions. Why you took what wasn't yours. Why you cut wires you shouldn't touch."

"I didn't cut wires," the older woman said, quick as a match struck. "I am many things, but I am not that careless."

"Then what did you do," Deena asked. She stood with her back to the aisle, one ear for the curtain, one ear for the room, every line alert.

"I opened a bin I shouldn't, because I wanted a squabble," Mrs. Carmichael said. "I whispered where whispers travel. I took a folder. I moved notes. I left a sentence where a temper would find it. I needed noise so the quiet work could be done."

"And the quiet work was what," Greta asked, pen poised.

"Deliver the coin to the right hands at the right time," Mrs. Carmichael said. "Keep the wrong heir from planting a flag in Paris."

"Who told you which hands were right," Amelia asked.

"A man who signed with an initial and thought that made him clean," Mrs. Carmichael said. "He wrote on paper that pretended to be older than it was. He borrowed words. He liked the way old menace sounded in a new throat."

"In your throat," Betsy said.

Mrs. Carmichael didn't flinch. "In mine," she said.

The Captain's voice sounded at a lower volume than before, a quiet confirmation that systems held. He didn't say the word safe. He didn't need to. The tone did the work.

Amelia laid out a neat row of items on a blue service cloth: the small blade in its napkin cradle, the sealed envelope they'd opened, the note inside, a photograph from Lionel's envelope showing a younger man by a pond. The edges of the photo were abraded, the gloss dulled by thumbs. On the back, in tidy script, the date and the name that had become a chant.

"Did 'A' send this," she asked.

"No," Mrs. Carmichael said. "A friend sent it years ago when we still wrote on paper because we were lonely, not because we were afraid."

"Why help him now," Greta asked. "Why not write to a court, or to the press, or to a daughter who could have talked you out of the knife."

Mrs. Carmichael's eyes softened at the last word. "I don't have a daughter," she said. "I have a file of letters that started with history and ended with debt. I have a pension that can vanish. I have a name that can be bent if someone holds it over the right flame."

"You were threatened," Amelia said.

"I was promised," Mrs. Carmichael said. "An end to something that burned longer than it ever made sense to burn."

"Then you met me in the dark," Amelia said.

"I tried to put a leash on the truth," Mrs. Carmichael said. "It does not wear one well."

Betsy shifted and lifted the trash bag a little higher, as if that tiny motion could lower the weight in the room. "He told you to grab the bait," she said. "Tonight."

"He told me to take any proof that didn't belong to the right line," Mrs. Carmichael said. "He told me that if his cousin failed, another would make noise, and that this time noise was the point."

"His cousin," Greta said, eyes narrowing on the pen.

"Yes," Mrs. Carmichael said, and the word landed without drama and with a great deal of meaning. "I am that cousin. Distant, through a line that left the manor before the wine was bottled for winter. That line left with a debt and a promise. He told me I could pay one and keep the other if I bent my back to the work."

"Describe the letters," Amelia said. "Paper, ink, where they came from."

"Blue airmail once, then brown envelopes with a French postmark, then a box from a shop in Piccadilly with a note inside tucked into the tissue," Mrs. Carmichael said. "Always the initial. Always the same phrases: 'broken promise,' 'blood debt,' 'final reconciliation.' It was like he thought I'd forget if he didn't make the words a chorus."

Greta's pen stopped moving. "The same phrases appear in Lionel's 1982 set," she said. "But the paper is different. The hand is different. The voice is an echo that thinks it's a bell."

Mrs. Carmichael looked at the photo again. "He wanted to be an echo you could touch," she said.

Deena's radio gave a small double click that meant the flight deck wanted quiet, not fear. She raised it to her mouth and murmured acknowledgment, then set it back on her hip. "Movement stays limited," she said over a shoulder. "We keep the aisle clear except for service."

"Service," Betsy perked. "I can pass water and not ask about blood debts once."

"Do that," Amelia said. "Soft voices. Low lights."

Betsy slipped through the curtain like a stage hand and emerged in the cabin with a smile that looked like home in an unfamiliar street. The murmur beyond dropped a notch. Cups knocked gently against rims. "Water?" Betsy asked. "Cookie?" A baby cooed at the glitter on her nails.

Amelia turned back to the counter. "Mrs. Carmichael," she said, "the device in the rear access was not you. The wires in the panel were not you. Did 'A' ask you to do anything mechanical at all."

"No," the older woman said. "He asked me to hurry. He asked me to give him back something he said was his. He asked me to tell him when others moved. He never trusted wires. He trusted paper and people who read it."

"Bradley trusts wires," Greta said quietly.

Amelia rolled the envelope between thumb and middle finger. The paper stuck for a second to the sweat on a knuckle. She could feel the groove the pen had carved through the strokes of the letter A. She could see the dot like a little black nail.

"What do you want now," she asked.

"I want to sleep," Mrs. Carmichael said. "I want to remember how a kitchen smells when the first peach of summer hits the cutting board. I want to walk my street and know the post brings news that doesn't use old words to do new harm."

"You'll have officers and questions first," Deena said. "Then peaches."

"I can answer questions," Mrs. Carmichael said. "I kept everything that wasn't light."

Greta flipped her pen in her fingers and then caught it, as if old habits could still be games. "The note we found in your pocket. How recent."

"This week," Mrs. Carmichael said. "It was waiting in my mailbox in a blank envelope with only my name, no return. I think someone placed it there by hand."

"Someone who knew where you live," Amelia said. "Who in this cabin knows where you live."

"None of them," Mrs. Carmichael said. "Some of them know the church I attend. Some know the school where I used to work. The letter knew my latch."

Air shifted through the vents. The plane's skin ticked in a way Amelia had learned to love. It meant life moved outside, thin air at speed, and inside, people who would never share a table on the ground shared air and time now. She leaned into that thought.

"Here's what happens next," she said. "We'll write a clear record: how the blade was found, how the folder was taken, what the note says. We'll put your purse under seal. We'll keep you here with water. You'll rest."

"I can't rest," Mrs. Carmichael said. "I have carried too much of this on my back for too long."

"You can set some of it down," Amelia said.

Betsy slipped back through the curtain with a flourish that ended in a whisper. "The honeymooners say thank you," she said. "Nolan asked if we have sparkling. I told him to imagine bubbles."

"Good," Deena said. "Keep them imagining."

Amelia took a breath that tasted like coffee and cabin air and the rubber band scent of restraint. She looked at the photograph again: a young man by a pond, jacket on his knees, the sun turning the water to brushed steel. The name on the back had become a spell that people used to justify old wants.

"Mrs. Carmichael," she said, "if we prove that the person who signs 'A' isn't Alastair at all, will you help us say so."

"Yes," the older woman said. "Even if saying it is the last thing I do for that name."

Greta's eyes shone, not with tears, but with the light of a solved line in a hard puzzle. "Then we'll work. And we'll do it without cutting any more wires."

A rustle in the curtain. Bradley's voice again, pressed through polite teeth. "I will be filing complaints," he said to no one who needed to hear it.

"We'll file things too," Deena muttered, and that small rise of humor steadied the room.

Amelia folded the note back into the envelope. She placed it in a clear bag and labeled the top in block print, the same way she labeled milk for carts or a list for crew: time, place, what, who. When she looked up, Mrs. Carmichael was watching her with something like relief.

"You'll keep it from getting dirty," the older woman said.

"That's the idea," Amelia said. She looked at the clock. "Paris is closer."

Mrs. Carmichael nodded. "He'll be there," she said. "If he didn't board, he'll still be there. Names like that always wait where bells ring."

"Then we'll be ready," Amelia said.

They were quiet for a while. In that quiet, the plane felt like a house where someone had finally opened a window after a long winter. Air moved. People slept. A few made lists on their phones and underlined words they never thought they'd care about.

"Amelia," Greta said, voice low. "When we're done here, we should compare the modern 'A' with the forged signature on the genealogy page. The styles are different, and that is a truth even paper can't hide."

"We'll do that," Amelia said. "And we'll do it right."

Betsy looked toward the aisle, judging mood the way some people judge weather from a weathervane. "We'll need one more water run," she said. "Then dim lights again."

"Make it happen," Deena said.

They moved with the same purpose they used during long flights when nothing happened and when too much did: small tasks done well, voices set to calm, eyes alive. The plane held them. The night agreed to let time pass.

When Amelia glanced back at the envelope one more time, the words seemed to grip harder than ink should. Fail me, and you fail the family. A threat. A dare. A bargain written by someone who loved power more than people.

She slid the bagged note into the service safe, locked the latch, and pressed two fingers to the metal to feel that it held.

"We keep going," she said again.

Mrs. Carmichael closed her eyes. "Thank you," she said, and it sounded like the kind of thank you you give to a person who has not forgiven you and somehow did not turn away.

Beyond the curtain, the aisle grew a little softer, a little kinder. Paris sat at the edge of the dark like a promise kept by strangers. The plane pointed its nose toward that light and stayed steady.

Chapter 19

The plane settled into a steady hush, a long exhale through vents that smelled of coffee and metal. The aisle lights glowed like a runway inside a tube of night. Amelia kept one palm on the galley counter, steadying herself on the low thrum, and laid the sealed note from "A" between a stack of paper cups and the crew log. Ink bled into the fibers. The letter felt warm from her pocket, as if a hand still pressed it from the other side.

Captain Reeves's voice floated from the interphone, a calm bar of tone that kept the cabin from fraying. Systems holding. No divert yet. Eyes up, stay present.

Betsy leaned close, whisper-small. "So we're chasing a ghost with a single letter for a face. That's fine. Low stakes."

Deena snorted. "You get two jokes. That was one."

"We need the pattern," Amelia said. "What they want isn't only the coin." She slid the sealed note back into an evidence sleeve and set it beside Greta's folder. "Carmichael's letters talk in circles. Someone else circles tighter."

Greta rested a palm on the metal counter. The bandage on her hairline peeked under her bangs. "The feud always paired objects. Marriage of proof with proof. A pledge and a seal. Split them and you split the claim."

"Two relics," Amelia said.

Greta nodded. "Coin and locket. A cameo. The crest repeats. Vine and riverbend."

Betsy widened her eyes. "You sat on that?"

"I wanted certainty."

"Welcome to coach," Betsy said. "We're fresh out."

Amelia switched from hush to action. "We verify with Lionel. If he can speak, we do it now."

They moved aft. The hum shifted timbre past the wing, a deeper undertow. Lionel sat propped in the last row behind a curtain, his blanket tucked to his ribs, the traveling physician on a jumpseat nearby with a cuff and a penlight. The small bruise on Lionel's forearm had darkened along the vein, a sour blueberry under the skin. His breath hitched at the cannula prongs.

"Can I ask a short question?" Amelia said to the physician.

"You get one," he said. "Two if they're good."

Amelia crouched. "Lionel. You told me there's a second piece. Not a coin. What is it?"

His eyes drifted, then anchored to hers. His voice scraped. "C...
cameo."

Greta leaned in. "The crest?"

He closed his eyes, opened them again. "Pairs... with the token.
Don't split." A cough shook him. "If split, claims twist." He swallowed. "Found, then... gone."

"Where?"

His gaze flicked toward the cabin, then down the aisle to the dark
seam where coach met the galley. "Here. Onboard."

Amelia squeezed his hand once, then stood. She felt the clock in
her chest shift from tick to sweep. "We search. Quiet. We do not
leave the cabin jumpy."

Deena moved beside her, jaw set. "I'll work the seat pockets. You
take bins and under-seats. Betsy floats and smiles."

"Copy," Betsy said. "I'm a mobile smile."

They split into lanes. The cabin looked like a sleeping field,
heads tilted, plastic cups gathered on armrests. Amelia eased open
bin doors in small arcs, like turning pages. Suitcases, a wool coat,
a box of macarons that rustled inside its ribbon. She slid fingers
along the lip of each bin, felt only dust and the tack of old cleaner.
She closed every latch with the same gentle pressure. Nothing
rattled. Nothing sang.

Row by row, Deena palmed seat pockets and returned loosed
earbuds, a pen, a paperback with swollen pages. Two rows up,
Nolan's eyes tracked her progress, then drifted to Rita's, who
squeezed his fingers and mouthed, breathe. He gave her a grin like
a paper cut, brave and thin.

Greta stayed one row behind Amelia with the crew manifest, tapping the corners of her photocopies, keeping a quiet cadence of names and seats. "If the cameo crossed hands in the blackout, the person didn't want to wave it. It would hide where fingers don't go. Under seats. Inside the fabric seam. Behind a kickplate."

"Lav?" Betsy asked.

"Not with everybody counting lav visits," Deena said from a crouch. "Whoever started the count in the first place wanted us to look there."

They reached the wing and crossed into the quieter back third, where the aisle narrowed and shoe tips pressed past one another in a slow shuffle whenever anyone stood. Amelia bent at each row and swept the under-seat with a flat palm. Gum beads, a stray peanut, the cool edge of metal seat rails. Her hand brushed something soft at 32D, the texture of velvet ground with dust. She stilled. Then she slid her fingers over the edge and pulled a small pouch into the aisle light.

Velvet, deep blue, flattened where weight had sat on it. A tie cord tangled around the mouth.

"Found," Amelia said.

Greta's inhale made a tremor at the edge of silence. Betsy bobbed, then steadied.

The man in 32D jerked upright. He had a quiet man's posture, spine bowed from hours of sitting small, eyes that watched the aisle while pretending they didn't. Lines radiated from his mouth like old wind. "What is that?" His voice bent toward a British cadence and then away, sanded to neutral.

Amelia loosened the cord and tipped the pouch. A cameo slid into her palm, warm from velvet. Carved shell. Profile in cream, a woman's throat and jaw alive with light. The crest wrapped the bezel: a river curve and a cluster of leaves, exactly as Greta had drawn with a ballpoint on a napkin hours before.

The cabin caught its breath without knowing why.

Greta lifted the locket by the chain and turned it in the light. "Authentic," she said. "The carving depth, the backfill, the clasp style. This is no tourist stall prize."

Betsy whispered, "We have both halves of the sword now."

"Not a sword," Greta said. "A pair of scales."

Bradley rose with a scrape of the seat track three rows forward. "You can't just hold that up like a game show," he said. "If it's real, it belongs to the rightful branch. Hand it to me or to Ms. Roth. We can—"

Tamsin stood, book cradled to her chest. "Not on your terms."

Bradley's smile set wrong in his face. "You burned your terms when you lied about knowing me. We all heard the honeymooners."

"I said we had contact. I didn't say we conspired." Her gaze fixed on the cameo, then on Greta. "We should not wave it. People bleed for less."

The man at 32D ran a hand over his pant leg, a stalling motion. "I've never seen that pouch," he said. "Not once. I don't know how it got under my seat."

"Which is not the same as saying you didn't put it there," Bradley said.

"Enough," Amelia said. "No one touches it." She cupped the cameo and the pouch together, like carrying a small bird. "We will keep the coin and the cameo together. That prevents more leverage plays."

Lionel's voice, thin but steady, drifted from the last row. "Keep them together." His hand trembled at the curtain edge. "If they split, the story splits."

Amelia met his eyes and nodded. "You have my word."

A murmur rippled. The older man in 32D stared at the locket as if it shone light on a page he'd hidden in a drawer. His throat worked. "Please," he said. "Put it away. People make choices they don't come back from."

"Like the choice to hide proof under your seat?" Bradley said.

The man's jaw tightened. "I told you."

Greta glanced between them. "What is your name, sir?"

"Har—" He stopped, the syllable catching. He rubbed his temple with two fingers and looked past Greta to Amelia. "I hoped this day would never crawl back through the window," he said. "I am Alastair's son."

A hush fell like a dropped blanket. The white noise of engines filled the space his words left.

Betsy blinked. "That would make you... I need a chart. I need all the charts."

Tamsin's mouth opened, then closed. She held her book tighter, knuckles pale. "Prove it," she said, voice quiet, iron under cloth.

Greta set the cameo back in the velvet and worked the tie tight, then slid the pouch into a crew evidence bag. She looked at the man in 32D. "Names matter. Dates matter. If you are who you say you are, you know the private marks. A place. A vow. Give me one anchor and I'll pull the line."

His gaze angled to the window where night pressed back in layers. "Not here," he said. "Not with all these eyes. I will say this. I was told to speak only if the worst arrived. I think the worst has taken a seat."

Amelia felt the cabin tilt, not with flight, with choice. She tucked the cameo in her apron pocket opposite the coin. Cold on one side, warm on the other. "Then you will sit, and you will not move without my eyes on you," she said. "Captain Reeves wants bodies in seats. He gets that. We sort the rest with our feet on the ground."

He nodded once. Whatever he kept behind his eyes didn't move.

Bradley hugged his arms across his chest. "We're just going to take a stranger's word for a dynasty?"

"We're going to land a plane full of people who want to see morning," Amelia said. "Then we will argue with paper and light."

Betsy let a breath out. "I like paper and light."

Deena clicked on the PA and gave coach a careful update about securing items and staying seated for the final night stretch. Her voice spread calm like warm air.

Amelia turned back to Lionel. "Together," she said again. She touched her apron pockets where the coin and cameo sat mirrored. He closed his eyes, as if that one word let him release a small muscle inside his chest.

A slow beat passed, just the engines and the quiet snick of a seat belt. Then the cabin's murmur began again, richer, threads of speculation weaving under the hum. Tamsin sank into her seat and opened her book without reading. Bradley didn't sit. He paced one step and back again, a caged motion, eyes on Row 32 as if he might pull words out of the man's mouth by force of glare alone.

Greta folded her copies, the edges aligned, a scholar sealing her thoughts. "We keep these together and we keep them moving," she said under her breath to Amelia. "Still water invites stones."

"Then we keep current," Amelia said. She set her shoulders, felt the coin and cameo balance her like ballast, and walked the aisle once more, checking faces she knew too well now, listening for the click of parts that didn't belong. Nothing clicked. But something leaned, ready to push.

They would be in Paris before dawn. That promise beat under every footfall. It also drew knives, the way a porch light draws moths. Amelia looked to 32D one last time. The man sat still, hands folded, head bowed. He had given them a single sentence and cracked the night in two.

They would need more than a sentence. They would need proof. They would need to keep breathing long enough to ask for it.

The plane hummed on, and the river in the crest, carved inside her apron pocket, seemed to curl forward in the dark.

Chapter 20

Cold air spilled from the vents as if the sky itself had opened a window. A metallic chime cut a thin line through the hush, and then another. Amelia stood in the forward galley with the captain's latest note card: two words in neat block print — expedite descent. She tucked the card against the ice drawer and turned to face the cluster in row 30 where the new claim had struck sparks.

The older man—Harold, he said at last—sat with his palms on his knees, eyes on the carpet. Tamsin occupied the aisle seat beside him like a checkpoint. Greta leaned into the row from across, notes braced on the armrest. Bradley hovered a few steps away, a storm with a tie clip.

Amelia knelt to Harold's eye level. "You said you're Alastair's son," she said. "We need one fact we can verify during flight. A name on a parish register. A location from a family story. Don't recite your whole life. Give us one nail."

His eyes lifted to hers, glassed with exhaustion and something that might have been regret. "I was born away from any register," he said. "A room above a bakery on Rue—" He stopped. "Above a bakery in Paris. The smell of yeast turned at dawn. Left-handed midwife with a scar where a ring once cut. That's what my mother told me." He swallowed. "It's not a nail. It's a breath."

"Sometimes a breath is a hinge," Greta said. "I have Carmichael's letters. There is a reference to a child born off the ledger. No street name. Only a turn by a church that also sold apples from a crate."

"Saint-Merri's small square," Harold said at once. His own certainty startled him. "Yes. The crate had blue paint."

Bradley laughed once, a bark. "We're litigating paint. Marvelous. This is why fortunes rot."

Tamsin's gaze never left Harold. "If you're true, you had time to tell the world. Why now?"

"I was told to wait. To be quiet unless the family tore itself down again," he said. "Then letters came. Threats. When I refused, Carmichael visited my home and left a photo on the stoop." His hands opened, empty. "Four faces circled. Mine was a corner of a jaw you could barely see."

"Photo with circles," Betsy said behind Amelia, flipping through a vinyl sleeve. "Got it. Three faces we know. Lionel. Tamsin's grandmother. Bradley's magazine headshot pasted. One is a ghost."

Greta's mouth pressed flat. "Carmichael baited him."

Amelia stood as the chime pinged twice. Her inner ear popped as the pressure shifted a hair. "We're beginning descent," she said to the row. "That means rules. Bodies in seats. Bags closed. Hands to yourselves. We're going to land if we keep our heads."

Deena's voice came over the PA, calm and level. "Ladies and gentlemen, we're starting our approach into Paris. Please return to your seats and fasten your belts. We'll be collecting any loose items."

A hiccup of movement at the front drew Amelia's eye. The curtain rippled in a draft. Someone had shifted near the cockpit corridor and vanished again. She tasted metal on the back of her tongue. The earlier hydraulics warning had passed, but the fuse that wanted attention still burned.

She split the problem. One track: people. One track: plane.

"Betsy," she said, "work the Carmichael notes for any mention of Harold. Proper nouns. Stamps. Postmarks."

"On it."

"Greta," Amelia said, "stay here with Tamsin and Harold. No relics leave my apron and no one touches my apron."

Greta nodded. "Consider me a fence."

"Bradley," Amelia said, turning, "sit down."

He didn't. "You put two relics in a flight attendant's pockets," he said. "That is your chain of custody?"

"It is the only chain I trust."

His lip curled, then smoothed into a customer-service smile that didn't touch his eyes. He sat anyway, but on the edge of the cushion, leaning forward as if he might spring.

The interphone buzzed. Amelia lifted it. "Hart."

Reeves kept his words short. "We're seeing a tweak on cabin pressure sensors. It's small. Could be sensor drift, could be someone with a screwdriver who wants to be famous. Keep your area locked down. We're descending on profile. If anything hisses where it shouldn't, call me."

"Copy."

She hung up and pulled Deena aside in the galley. "We have a tickle on pressure. Check the aft access point. Don't touch anything you don't have to. Eyes only."

Deena nodded and moved in a low, fast walk. Betsy slid into her space at the counter and opened Carmichael's notebook. "No index. Just fury and glue."

"Fury first, then glue," Amelia said.

Pages flipped. Betsy tapped a margin. "Here. 'The child born in secrecy.' No name. Then a code letter 'H.' And this note: 'If he refuses, bring him to the light.' H for Harold, maybe. Or H for a lie."

"It's enough to hold him as possible," Greta said from the row.

A shiver ran down the cabin. Not cold. A ripple of energy when a lot of people start thinking the same thought. Passengers craned toward the windows where nothing yet showed but the dense dark over the Atlantic. A baby let out a curious squeak and then, as if surprised by its own voice, went quiet. The plane trimmed its nose.

Ears popped row by row. Bottles chimed in carts as if they were small bells for a service no one wanted.

Tamsin rose half out of her seat, then forced herself back down. "I want to see the cameo."

"You can look," Amelia said, "from there." She took out the evidence bag long enough for the profile to catch the aisle light. Then she slipped it back. "We land with both. Together."

Harold let out a breath that shook. "My mother said the crest's river curve came from the land itself," he said. "A little bend where the vineyard meets a stream. She said you could hear the water if you held the seal near your ear."

"We'll go listen when we're on ground," Betsy said. "We'll listen to a fountain and pretend."

Bradley stood again. "You're playing house. Hand it to me, or to Ms. Roth, or to the captain. Someone with skin in the line."

Greta leaned over the aisle. "Your skin is the line," she said. "That's been clear all night."

He took a step toward her row. Nolan's call light blinked two rows behind him. Amelia moved to intercept, but Deena's voice crackled in her ear over the crew line. "Aft access panel shows tool flare on two screws. Someone tried to get under it and thought better."

"Any device?"

"None. But there's a scuff on the vinyl like a knee knelt hard."

"Copy. Strap in for landing but keep your eyes free."

A low announcement rolled down the cabin from the flight deck. "Flight attendants, prepare for landing." It carried the calm weight of a promise. All over the plane, belts clicked and arms pulled blankets up. Heads leaned back. Harold pressed his hands together and touched them to his lips, a wordless request into the seams of the world.

Tamsin turned on him. "If you're true, you waited decades while others fought. People died. Why stay silent?"

"Silence felt like mercy at first," he said. "Then it felt like a trap. I'm sorry." He looked toward Amelia. "I didn't want this night."

"None of us booked it," Betsy said.

A woman across the aisle hissed at her spouse to stop filming. He lowered his phone with a grudging shrug. Amelia caught his eye. He reddened and tucked it away.

The nose dipped a little more. Paris lay ahead like a thought about to form.

Bradley couldn't hold still. He took two steps down the aisle and spoke low, the kind of voice that uses privacy like a knife. "Ms. Roth," he said, "tell them the truth. You approached me. You begged for my help."

Tamsin kept her eyes on Harold. "I asked you to stop sending people to my door."

"You asked me to make the papers go away."

"I asked you to stop forging them."

He laughed again, too loud. Heads turned. "Accusation as defense. Classic."

Greta lifted a hand for quiet. "Both of you save it. We have to land."

A hiss, soft and wrong, brushed the back of Amelia's neck from the forward galley. Not in the ducts. Close. She pivoted, lifted the curtain, and found the service door's trim rattling a hair, not from airspeed. A piece of tape that had sealed a corner earlier hung loose, the edge curling like a leaf. She pressed it flat and felt a tiny breath of air where no air should move. Not a breach. A whisper.

She checked the latch indicator. Green. Safe. But someone had tugged at a seam to make a captain nervous.

The interphone buzzed in her hand before she called. "Hart," she said.

Reeves again. "We see the same tickle but nothing out of limits. We're landing in under fifteen. Keep all the drama behind your curtain."

"Working on it."

When she turned, Ms. Roth had stepped into the aisle with the poise of a woman who knows a courtroom is only a room. She faced Harold and held up the cameo in its bag, her palm under it like a scale. "You claim this because you say a woman I never met slept with a man I never met," she said. "That's wind. I want stone. Give me one stone."

Harold looked as if she had asked him to raise a building with his hands. "The photo," he said. "Pull back the tape on the back and you'll find the penciled initials in a hand that isn't mine."

Betsy already had the vinyl sleeve open. She slid the circled-face photo free and turned it over. There, in graphite worn pale by decades, a set of initials with a date: A.R., 1965. She looked up.

"Alastair de Riviere," she said. "And a year that matches the label on Tamsin's photo."

Tamsin's breath caught. "I have that photo in my bag. Different copy. Same face. Same date."

Greta took both images and laid them side by side on the tray table. "Paper stock matches period. Tearing patterns are cousins, not twins. Two prints made from one negative." She nodded once. "This is a stone."

Bradley's jaw ticked. "Nice trick," he said. "You all pat yourselves and still no one proves he's that man's son. You need blood, not paper."

"Blood follows paper in court," Greta said.

"Blood follows knives in aisles," Amelia said. "Sit down."

He didn't. He edged toward the galley again, eyes on Amelia's apron. The look had heat and calculation both. She could see him mapping a path between elbows and armrests. Deena's voice crackled in her ear again, a thin wire of sound. "Galley rear secure. Keep your head, Ame."

"I always do," she said, and that won a quick, bent smile from Betsy.

The lights dropped to a softer night mode for approach, then flicked brighter for checks. Shadows sharpened, then softened again. People braced even when they didn't mean to, shoulders higher under sweaters.

The interphone buzzed again, a burst of static on the crew line. Then a voice that wasn't Reeves, wrapped in fabric, pressed through. Low. Not a growl. A hiss made of words. "Stop the theater. That cameo is mine."

Amelia's skin prickled. The voice wasn't in her ear. It came from the forward galley itself, a whisper laid exactly by the curtain gap. She stepped through.

The narrow space pinched around her. Racks, boxes, the faint sweet of juice. From the shadow by the service cart a figure stepped out, face covered by a black cloth mask cut from a T-shirt. Taller than most in coach, shoulders set square. In his fist, a shard of torn metal from a galley rack, edges jagged, glinting in the light like a cruel idea.

"Hand over the cameo," the figure said. The mask made the voice dull. "You have five seconds to be smart."

Amelia held her ground. The apron tugged at her neck from the weight of both pieces. Past the attacker, the curtain breathed with the ship, a small pulse. Behind her, the cabin held its fear like air for a dive.

"I'm not handing anything to a mask," she said. "Step back and the captain will put us on the ground without extra sirens."

The shard lifted a fraction. The figure took one step closer, the shoes whispering over the mat. The breath that reached her through the cloth had the smell of coffee and a bite of mint.

"Your time," the voice said, "is over."

Amelia slid her heel back to lock herself against the trolley, shoulders squared, eyes never leaving the cut metal. "My time," she said, "is landing this plane alive."

The figure tilted his head as if the line amused him. The shard moved again, a small readjustment for a better angle.

Behind the curtain, the cabin belts clicked like rain. Paris drew nearer, a city of stone and paper waiting to see who would step into that light with a true name.

The shard rose. The mask breathed. And the galley seemed to shrink to the size of a glove box with two people and an old war squeezed into it.

"Hand it over," the figure said. "Or the world reads a headline you'll never see."

Chapter 21

The galley smelled like scorched coffee and lemon wipes. Metal hummed underfoot. The curtain breathed with the pressurized air as if the plane itself took slow, measured breaths.

"Hand over the cameo," the masked figure said.

Amelia kept her hands loose, palms open. The locket sat behind her on the ice drawer, velvet pouch tucked under a towel. She kept her eyes on the jagged strip of metal in the figure's fist. It had the dulled shine of a tool that had scraped where it never should.

"You do not want to do this," she said. "We are about to land. The cabin is watching. Put that down, and we end this without more harm."

A laugh came through the cloth, tight, a rough scrape in the throat. "You have no idea what is owed. You move, I cut."

The engines droned steady. The deck tilted by a hair. Amelia took the air in the way she always did when a tray threatened to tip—small, clean, ready for a catch. She shifted her weight enough to feel the latch of the cart at the back of her calf.

"Talk to me," she said. "What is the rush now, after hours of fear? If you want the locket, you need to tell me why."

"It is mine," the voice said. "By right. By loss. By every lie the others told."

The cadence was familiar. The vowels clipped a certain way. The last consonant hit like a gavel, not a sigh. She pictured a man barking about connections, about a deal, about a crisis. She heard him in the aisle sniping at every delay. She heard him in row bickering, not just angry—hungry.

Amelia kept him going. "By whose name?"

"By de Riviere," he said. "And by the name your little historian would carve off the tree if she could."

She let the space hang for one beat, then another. The plane dipped a breath and rose again. A drawer slid a finger along its track and stopped. The mask hid his face, but a stripe of pale skin showed across the knuckles that gripped the metal.

"Bradley," she said.

He flinched.

"You have been loud all night," she said. "Always the victim. Always the clock. Always the one who needs this flight to hurry for a crisis that never had a name. That voice gave you away."

His shoulders squared. The strip of metal lifted a hair. Behind Amelia, ice cracked in a bucket as it settled.

The curtain behind the attacker shook. Betsy's wide eyes appeared in the narrow seam for half a breath, then vanished. Good. Help had not rushed in. Help had gone to get more help.

"You will not stall me," he said. He stepped closer. The edge of metal kissed the towel.

"Then no more stalling," Amelia said. "You want the locket. You say it is yours. You say the others lied. Tell me what you did to earn it. Tell me why Mrs. Carmichael ran errands for you."

"Carmichael was weak," he said. "Years of letters and still no nerve. I gave her the push she needed. She owed our line. She owed me."

"You pushed a grandmother into a blade," Amelia said. "You shoved a historian into a wall. You laced wires in the PA panel with a tool from your kit. And the coin has fresh scratches that match that same edge."

He cocked his head. The mask cut a flat mouth where his jaw set. "Prove it."

"Your kit sat under 14C with tape over the name," she said. "Deena has it now. Captain Reeves has the device from the rear access. The marks match. The coin carries a new crescent, not from time, from a hand that wanted chaos."

"You are a flight attendant," he said. "Not a judge. Not a cop. Hand the locket over."

The interphone clicked at her hip. A soft chime. The captain's voice rode the wire. "Cabin crew, five minutes," he said. "Field in sight." Calm, balanced, like water poured along a lip without a drip.

Amelia held Bradley's gaze. "You tried to pin your work on Tamsin," she said. "You said she would leap ahead. You said she was the granddaughter. You screamed that she was the thief."

"She is the thief," he said. He pushed nearer. Heat came off him like a body rushed up a flight of stairs. "She called on that teacher to dig up what should have stayed buried. She led Carmichael to me."

Amelia kept her hands wide. "She is many things," she said. "But the tool marks do not lie. Your temper does not lie. The forged signature in Greta's stack does not lie either. The modern 'A.' with a clean nib. The ink fresh enough to shine."

"You think I wrote that?" he said. "The tree needed a pruning to keep dead limbs from stealing fruit. Everyone on this plane wants a harvest. I did what had to be done."

"Then take off the mask," Amelia said. "Look at me and say that."

His shoulders rose and fell twice. The strip of metal twitched. He reached up with his free hand and tore the mask away.

Sweat beaded along his hairline. His eyes had the look of a cornered dog. His lip curled like a match with a bend.

"You want truth," he said. "Fine. I staged enough noise to buy time. I needed the coin. I needed the locket. With both, the claim shifts. The museum pays to prevent a scandal. Or a court pays. Either way, I stop bleeding cash. Either way, my name matters when we hit Paris."

"You used Carmichael," Amelia said.

"She came preloaded with guilt," he said. "A cousin always ready to serve some noble shade. I sent the notes. I fed her lines. She thought she served a ghost. She served me."

A shape moved at the curtain seam. Greta's bandage sat white against her hair. Tamsin's profile hovered behind her. Harold's coat brushed the rail.

"Bradley," Greta said from the threshold. "You taught yourself the family tree from a teenager's notebook. You learned the coat of arms to pitch money men on a fake exhibit. You learned just enough French to sound like you belonged near a door marked crew only. That is not blood. That is a con."

"Stay back," Bradley snapped. He swung the metal in a short arc. The tip nicked the towel and sliced a thin line.

Tamsin stepped out from behind Greta. "You tried to ruin me," she said. "You lied to that teacher in letters with my name at the bottom. You handed the press a file with my grandmother's photo and a caption I never wrote."

"You were noise," he said. "You were leverage. You were the cover if this went bad. All of you were covers. The old man who claims he is a son, the scholar, the cousin—noise."

A seat belt ping ran the length of the cabin. The deck changed pitch. The air pressed harder in the ears.

Amelia inched a foot closer to the ice drawer. "Bradley," she said. "Listen to the engines. We are almost down. This ends with the locket logged and you in cuffs. Or it ends with more harm. Do not make the second choice."

His jaw worked. His eyes cut to the towel. His hand flexed.

A soft cough came from the corridor. Lionel stood there with Deena's arm under his. He looked like a man held to the present by will. His face had no color. His fingers trembled.

"Bradley," Lionel said. "You do not have a claim."

Bradley's laugh cracked like a plate. "You can barely stand."

"I can stand long enough," Lionel said. Deena's hand hovered behind his elbow without touching. "You forged a tree, then you pruned it to fit your story. You erased names. You added a signature that never existed. You still missed the letter that tied the cameo to the coin under a single holder until settlement."

He lifted a folded sheet, careful, like a nurse handling a burn. "Here," Lionel said. "The other half of the proof you could not find. It sat in my jacket hem."

Bradley's eyes darted between the towel and the paper. Greed tugged his head toward both at once. He twitched forward.

Amelia slid her hip against the ice drawer and blocked the towel with her thigh.

"Read it," Lionel said. His breath hitched. He swallowed. "Read where your name sits in the margin from 1982 with the words witness only. Read where my father's contact refused your line the right to hold both pieces. Read the clause that binds the coin and the locket to one chain until a court in Paris can see them together."

Bradley took another step. "Give it."

"Come take it," Lionel said. He held the page toward the galley light. The paper quivered like a leaf. "You will still lose."

Harold edged along the other side of the curtain, palm up, voice quiet. "Son, stand down," he said. "The field is near. None of this will move your case forward. We will sort names with the police."

"I am not your son," Bradley said without looking. "You are another liar who stepped forward at the last minute because a teacher begged you to save her pride."

Harold lowered his hand, not in defeat, in measure. He kept himself between the blade and Greta without crowding Bradley. "We will deal with my part as well," he said. "But not with a blade in the air."

Another chime. "Cabin crew, two minutes," the captain said.

Bradley lunged.

The blade flashed and clinked off the drawer rail. Amelia moved. She threw the towel up into his face. The scent of lemon flooded her nose. She drove her shoulder into his chest and hooked her foot behind his ankle. He stumbled. The metal strip skittered under the cart.

The locket pouch bumped the floor and bounced into the aisle. It rolled and rested against Tamsin's shoe.

Bradley twisted like a man who had trained his body for squash and never for a fight. He lashed out, caught Lionel's sleeve, tore the page free by a corner, and ripped it down the fold.

"Hey," Betsy shouted from the curtain. "Hands off the archives."

Greta darted low and scooped the fallen half. Tamsin knelt and cupped the pouch. She slid the locket into her palm with care fit for something alive. She met Amelia's eyes for a beat. No plea. No claim. Just a silent question.

Amelia nodded once toward her own apron pocket.

Tamsin crossed the space in two quick steps and pressed the locket into Amelia's hand. Amelia tucked it into the pocket and snapped the button.

Bradley threw his weight at the pocket. Amelia pivoted and gave him hip and elbow. He slammed into the side of the cart. The cart wheel bumped over the metal strip on the floor and locked.

"Enough," Deena said. Her voice cut like the captain's. She hooked Bradley's wrist with a practiced motion from years of self-defense refreshers and pinched two nerves that turned his grip to water.

Harold took the other arm. Greta slid the blade away with her shoe. Betsy crouched on the metal strip so it could not slide.

Bradley fought like a man who knew fights always work when you are bigger and louder. They did not work here. Not in a narrow space with a cart at one hip and a wall at the other and four people who cared more about a full plane than any old feud.

"Let go," he snarled. Spit flecked his chin. "You fools don't understand money. You don't understand what a court can do when the right people are paid to read the right way."

"Courts read," Greta said. "Money argues. Evidence wins. You never had all of it."

Lionel leaned against the bulkhead, drawing breath like a bellows with a split seam. "He injected me," he whispered.

Amelia looked over Bradley's shoulder and met Lionel's eyes. He tapped the bruise on his forearm, then let his hand fall. "During the flicker. Small tool. Fast stick."

"We will pass that to the medics," Amelia said.

Bradley jerked again for the pocket. Deena torqued his wrist. He groaned and sank to a knee.

"Captain," Amelia said into the interphone, breath steady, words clipped. "Offender restrained. Locket secured. Count stable."

"Copy," the captain said. "One minute."

The plane's nose trimmed down. Wheels rolled forward from the bays with a low drumbeat. The city spread below them, a mesh of lights under a thin skin of cloud. The air pressed the cabin. Ears popped in little clicks.

Greta held her half of the torn page and brought it to Lionel. He pressed it to the other half in his hand. The tear fit like cut cloth. Together the clauses formed a loop that left no gap.

"Photos," Betsy said, already lifting her phone, then catching herself. "After the police," she amended, cheeks pink.

Harold looked at the mask that lay in the corner. "End this," he said to Bradley. "Stand and walk off this plane with a shred of grace."

Bradley bared his teeth. "Give me the locket."

"No," Amelia said.

The runway rose toward them. A ripple built under the floor.

Amelia glanced down the aisle. Passengers craned, then tried not to look. Hands covered mouths. Eyes leaned over armrests and then turned away out of respect, or fear, or both. Rita held Nolan's hand. Nolan had his free hand on the buckle like a man who planned to obey a sign for once in his life. Ms. Roth's book sat forgotten in her seat pocket, a ribbon of paper marking a page about civil law and impossible names.

The wheels hit with a bounce. The cabin shook. A cheer caught in some throats and stayed there when they saw the galley.

"Ladies and gentlemen," the captain said, voice calm as ever, "welcome to Paris. Please remain seated with your belts fastened."

Sirens stitched blue across the window slats as they rolled. The plane slowed. The hum dropped to a purr.

Amelia let the air go out of her lungs in one long thread. She looked at Bradley. Sweat ran at his temple. He had the set of a man who understood that math had turned against him. Tools on him. Mask on the floor. Ink on a page that did not match his story. Witnesses on all sides. A chain that linked coin and locket under a rule older than him.

"Hands," Deena said. She pulled flex cuffs from the drawer. "Wrists together."

He obeyed. Not out of kindness. Out of physics.

The door to the bridge opened with a hiss. Blue jackets waited there, faces unreadable, bodies square.

Amelia pressed her palm against the pocket where the locket rested. She let her fingers feel the shape for one small second. Not as treasure. As evidence. As a symbol ready to leave a long, bad night.

She found Lionel's gaze again. He gave her the ghost of a nod. The kind a man gives when he has outlived a storm he thought might swallow him whole.

The plane eased to the gate. The chime sounded for the last time. They had made it.

CHAPTER TWENTY-TWO

Chapter 22

Blue strobes washed the cabin as officers stepped through the door and took the aisle in that quiet, purposeful way that made everything else fade. The smell of jet fuel bled in at the threshold. For a beat, the plane felt like a sealed chapel with steel ribs, lit by emergency light, filled with the hush of a congregation that had seen enough.

Bradley came first, wrists bound, head lowered. The officers took him without a word, turned him smoothly, then led him forward. He threw a last look toward Amelia. Not a plea. An old grudge without an address.

Mrs. Carmichael followed in a wheelchair pushed by a paramedic. The blanket lay high on her lap. Her hands shook on top of it. She stared at the floor as if answers might be written in the scuffs. Greta touched the blanket edge as it passed, not to forgive and not to scold, only to mark that they had all shared the same air for a long long night.

Captain Reeves gave brief statements at the front under the watch of a uniform with a notebook. His face held the same still water it always held when the plane bucked or the radio crackled. He pointed the officers to the rear galley, to the panel with frayed wire tips, to the drawer where Deena had set a zip tie roll, to the small bag where the metal strip now lay tagged.

Passengers rose by row under Deena's direction. The door chime clinked. People stepped off in a line that moved like a river after a dam cracked open. Rita clung to Nolan's hand, then let go, then took it again. Nolan stared at the wing with the look of a man who had found religion in the physics of lift.

"Wait one," Betsy said to Amelia, lifting her phone. "Proof that we survived." She leaned in, eyes bright, then lowered the phone before the flash. "Later," she said. "Right. Police first, selfies second."

Amelia gave her a small smile. "Third," she said. "Coffee."

"Fourth," Betsy said, "sleep for a week."

Harold stood near row 32 with his coat folded over his forearm. He looked smaller without a claim on his tongue. Tamsin stood across from him with her book pressed flat against her ribs.

"Ms. Roth," Harold said. "I was not ready to say what I said. I do not know the whole of it. I only know a piece."

Tamsin nodded. "Then say the piece," she said. "Say it to a recorder. Say it to a lawyer who knows the old language. Say it to Greta. Say it where no one can twist it by force or threat."

Harold's mouth tightened. He looked at the floor. He lifted his gaze to Amelia. "You kept us alive," he said.

"We all kept each other alive," Amelia said. "It took a crowd."

Greta arrived with the torn page sealed in a clear sleeve. "You can both help close this," she said. "Not win it. Close it. A museum case is kinder than a courtroom for family bones."

Tamsin exhaled. "I do not need a throne," she said. "I need the feud to stop writing to strangers."

Harold's eyes warmed by a degree. "Truce until paper says otherwise," he said, and held out his hand.

Tamsin took it. The shake looked like two people who had both been children once, both scolded for things they did not do, both told that names meant more than faces.

Deena touched Amelia's shoulder. "Statements," she said. "Then we rest."

At the aft galley a young officer with a square jaw and soft eyes lifted a pen. "Name," he said. "Role on board. Describe what you saw." The word saw belonged to his form, not to Amelia's mouth. She walked him through the night: the coin glint, the blackout, Lionel's collapse, Greta's injury, the notes, the threats, the panel, the device, the letters from 1982, the forged signature, the final lunge in the galley.

He took it in without a single theatrical twitch. When she finished, he checked his boxes and nodded. "The locket," he said.

Amelia reached into her apron pocket, unbuttoned the flap, and drew the pouch into the galley light. The cameo slid into her palm, creamy oval, crest sunk like a thumbprint in history. It did not look like money. It looked like a promise that had failed a family for a long time.

Greta held out a museum evidence bag. The officer read out a number. Another officer wrote the number down on a clipboard. The bag sealed. The cameo passed from hand to hand with enough care to embarrass any storm.

"And the coin," the officer said.

Lionel had the pouch under the blanket on his stretcher. He lifted it with both hands, like a father who had learned to hold weight with tender fingers. He looked at Amelia. She nodded.

"It belongs where the fight ends," he said. "Not where it starts."

"Do you consent to transfer to police custody," the officer asked, "for eventual handoff to the proper registry with Dr. Morrison logged as consulting historian?"

Lionel's smile touched one corner of his mouth. "That is a sentence I will frame," he said. "Yes."

The officer logged both pieces. Greta signed as consultant. Captain Reeves signed as witness. Amelia signed as chain-of-custody. The ink dried under the galley light in neat rows.

A medic leaned in toward Lionel. "We have a bed ready," she said. "You will be fine, sir. We will check that bruise, draw labs, make sure no one put anything in you that should not be there."

Lionel's eyes closed for one breath, then opened. "I will answer questions after a nap," he said, and earned a small laugh from the medic.

Passengers still filtered off. The cabin lost coats and bags and whispers. The rows took on that picked-over look a plane gets after a long day: wrappers in pockets, a scarf in a crack, a water cup kept as a talisman because someone thought the water had special luck in it.

Betsy drifted by with Nolan and Rita. "If you ever write a manual for flying through madness," Betsy said, "put a chapter in there about lemon wipes."

"Chapter one," Amelia said, "wash your hands."

"Chapter two," Nolan said, "buckle the belt the first time she asks."

Rita lifted her wrist and showed a pink mark from the strap after the rough air. "Worth it," she said. "We get a story for the kids. Without the part where anyone dies."

"Best kind of story," Amelia said.

They went out into the bright gate. New passengers waited beyond the rope line with eyes on phones and bags at feet, unaware that the steel heart of this plane had raced all night and still made it home.

Amelia moved down the aisle with a trash bag and a rag because that is what you do after adrenaline flies off. You wipe a tray. You pull a napkin from a hinge. You tuck a seatbelt back across a cushion. You restore the small things so the big things do not swallow you.

Deena appeared beside her with a bottle of water. "Drink," she said. "Then answer two more questions for the officer who likes neat forms, then bed."

"Deal," Amelia said.

Greta lingered at row 25, hand on the seatback where the letter had been wedged. She stood still a long time. "They wrote rage on paper in 1982," she said to no one in particular. "Tonight we wrote a ceasefire in blue ink. That feels like a better use of hands."

"You earned your coffee," Deena said to her.

"If I drink more coffee," Greta said, "I will meet God."

Betsy popped back in with her phone now that the police had released the cabin. "Now," she said, "one photo. Not for the internet. For the quiet drawer at home where I put plane napkins and ticket stubs."

They crowded in near the aft galley: Amelia, Deena, Greta with a faint smile, Harold with a wary one, Tamsin with the book now closed and held by her side, Lionel propped on the stretcher like a tired king in a hoodie, Betsy in the foreground doing a peace sign, then catching herself and dropping it because tonight had not been peace but something more stubborn.

Click.

"Thank you," Betsy said.

The officers taped a square of the aisle where the metal strip had scraped the floor. They bagged the mask. They bagged the tool. They took a small swab from the PA panel. They spoke to each other in quiet half-sentences. The plane took on that half-sleep that comes after effort, the sound of fabric and zippers and pens.

Forms complete, the officer with the square jaw handed a receipt to Greta. "Evidence logged," he said. "Dr. Morrison, we will contact you for expert notes. Ms. Hart, the airline will get a copy of the full report. Mr. Hughes, we will visit the hospital as soon as you are settled."

"Thank you," Amelia said.

He nodded to all of them. "Thank you for keeping a lid on a pot that wanted to boil."

When the last passenger rolled down the jet bridge and the noise outside dropped by a degree, the plane felt like a room you know in the dark. Amelia stood in the aisle and listened to it breathe. She pressed her palm to the bulkhead the way mechanics do when they like a machine. The metal gave her back the cool of the night and the shake of landing, but also something like a heartbeat. Or maybe that was just her own.

Deena came back from the door and leaned her shoulder into Amelia's. "You okay?"

"I am," Amelia said. "Hungry. I would eat a bread roll older than me."

Deena laughed. "Let's not test that."

A radio chirped. A ground agent asked to clear the cabin for a full sweep. The officers gave the go-ahead. Evidence flags dotted the galley like small sunflowers with numbers.

Greta looked at the cameo in its bag and the coin in its bag and let her fingers rest on the plastic without pressing. "Glass and placard," she said. "No more knives. No more wires. Just light and a line of school kids and an old guard who tells them that grown-ups once fought over this and then stopped."

Tamsin stood with her arms crossed for warmth. "If there is a plaque," she said, "put every name on it. The ones who tried to cheat and the ones who tried to fix it. Truth works better when it is not polite."

Harold nodded. "I will come read it," he said. "If I can do that without anyone spitting."

"I will stand next to you," Tamsin said. "They can spit at both of us and then get bored."

They smiled at each other. Small. Real.

At last the aisle emptied. The blue lights were gone from the windows. The police tape came down. The captain shook hands with the officers and then with Amelia and then with Deena, the way a man thanks his crew on any night that ends on a runway and not in a headline.

"Good work," he said. "File when you wake."

"Yes, sir," Amelia said.

She took one more turn through the cabin. Two blankets folded. One pair of earbuds coiled. One book in a seat pocket with a library stamp, which she carried up front for the lost-and-found bin. She paused by row 25 and looked at the crack where the old letter had slept.

She stood on the jet bridge for a second before stepping off, letting the airport air hit her face, sharp with cold and rubber and new promise.

Deena squeezed her shoulder. "Paris," she said, and tilted her head toward the terminal glass where night held a city full of bread and sirens and people who were already up for work.

"Paris," Amelia said. "I just wanted a routine red eye."

She smiled. Not a big smile. The kind a person saves for themselves when the lights come up after a long, strange show. Then she walked toward the glow and the doors that opened with a soft hiss, ready to hand off the night and let the day take it.

Printed in Dunstable, United Kingdom

67765431R00122